A Thousand Piece Puzzle

A Thousand Piece Puzzle

Candace Pannell

Puzzle Publishing Co.

PO Box 16109
High Point, NC 27261

A Thousand Piece Puzzle

ISBN 10: 0-69276-800-9
ISBN 13: 978-0-69276-800-6

First Printing August 2016
Printed in the United States of America

10 9 8 7 6 5 4 3 2 1

DEDICATION

I want to dedicate this book to every person who may have experienced pain in a relationship . Hoping that this book will inspire others that pain does not last always. Although change in ones life may feel confusing, most of the time it is for the best.

Chapter One

Love is similar to a thousand-piece puzzle; only a select few will take the time and patience to focus on putting it together. A smaller percentage of people will take the time to frame it and treasure it for a lifetime. Will I, being so dim and broken, one day find the strength to put my puzzle together? Only time will tell.

October 15, 2015 4:18pm

"Damn…." "I need another phone." The current phone that I have is on my ex's plan and I know he's monitoring every call and text that I make. When I get off of work today I am going by the Sprint store. I've just got to get my own plan. I hope they have the new IPhone in the rose gold color. Yes, I am quite the Apple junkie. I've been separated from my ex since June 2014, although my marriage really ended months before. I prayed that things would get better but deep down inside I knew that I couldn't stay in it.

"Why is Wendover so busy?" I said to myself as I sat at the stoplight by the Red Lobster in Greensboro, North Carolina. It was 5:20pm and I was sitting in bumper-to-bumper traffic. Finally traffic began moving. I pulled into the parking lot of the Sprint store. Wow! This place is packed like always. I just knew I would be waiting forever. A nice young gentleman, dark skinned and easy on the eyes greeted me.

"Hi my name is Sidal. May I have your name please?"

"Hi Sidal I'm Paris"

Sidal smiled and placed my name on the list. I started to look around and glanced at their IPhone display. "Yes." "That is the one I want, the new IPhone." I thought to myself. I didn't have to wait long. Sidal came and assisted me in a very short period of time. While I applied for the phone another nice gentleman walked over to greet me.

"Mrs. James…" He extended his hand. When I made eye contact I realized whom this man was.

"Bradd…" "How are you? I haven't seen you in forever…" Bradd was a very handsome man with very prominent features, lips, nose, & the cutest light brown eyes. I was very attracted to him and had actually been attracted to him since we met. We used to work together years ago in the financial industry. I see we both had made different moves career wise. He was about 5'10", very muscular with a very full, rough beard and the sexiest deep voice you would want to hear. He made it known that he was interested by the way he caressed my hand and gazed into my eyes. His actions pretty much told me exactly how he felt. Sidal continued to assist me with obtaining my IPhone, gave me a discount through my employer and signed me up on the forever plan. Since the phones were on backorder Sidal said he would call me whenever it came in.

Such a long day, I climbed in my car and headed to my mother's house. She had agreed to watch my kids so I could go straight to the Sprint store from work. In about twenty minutes I pulled up in her driveway and beeped my horn. She had been expecting me so the kids flew out in no time.

"How are you guys doing? Did you have a good time at grandma's?" I asked.

Simone answered, "I'm fine ma, I had a really good time. Grandma let us play outside and then called us in for fried chicken and collard greens."

"Yes we had a good time and I'm stuffed. She sent you a plate mom." Sammy said.

I glanced up and saw my mom standing on her porch. I rolled down my window and shouted, "Thanks ma, love you!" She waved and went back into her house. On the way home one of my favorite songs started to play on the radio. I was tuned into 1075 KZL with Jared and Katie in the morning. They were hosting a twenty-four hour show to raise money for Family Services of the Piedmont, which focused on many agency programs including domestic violence shelters & family preservation. David Guetta's Titanium featuring Sia began to play. This song gave me so much inspiration and confidence to realize my own inner strength. Before I knew it my eyes began to fill with tears. I looked in my rearview mirror to check on the kids. They had fallen asleep during the ride home. We finally arrived home at 9:11pm. I pulled into the well lit parking deck of my condo.

"Alright kids time to wake up" I said.

"Shower then bed, because you all have school tomorrow." We took the elevator to the 11th floor. I opened the door and the kids rushed down the hall to get ready for bed. I walked into my bathroom and turned on the shower. I really enjoyed taking long hot showers & baths. I found them to be the one thing that actually worked for me at relieving stress. I walked back to the hall to ensure that the kids were actually getting ready for bed.

My kids were very well behaved and normally followed the directions that they were given. I didn't have my youngest daughter with me; her father and I alternate weeks with her. My oldest Sammy was already in the shower and his sister Simone was picking out her school clothes for the next day. After my separation from Jasper, I had decided to downsize tremendously. I owned a small three-bedroom condo at Center Pointe located downtown Greensboro at the intersection of West Friendly Avenue and Elm Street. It overlooked the city of Greensboro. It was very affordable compared to the prices in Washington, DC. I had decorated the girl's room in pink and white. The room was painted white & had a light pink and white vertical striped accent wall, white wooden bunk beds with downy soft white duvets. My daughter Simone was quite the artist. I actually used a few pieces of her artwork from school, framed them and placed them on the wall. Sammy's room on the other hand was the total opposite. He enjoyed sports and books. His favorite team was the Seattle Seahawks. In his room was an oak bunk bed with of course, Seahawk bedding. A desk sat in the corner of his room with a football lamp and his MacBook for doing research for his school projects.

I walked back into my bedroom, found my nightstand that I kept all of my Adult toys in, grabbed the bullet and headed back to the shower. The bathroom had become so steamy that I could hardly see my reflection in the mirror I pulled my pale pink chiffon blouse over my head, tugged my black dress pants down from around my wide hips, unsnapped my pink and white lace bra, threw it on the floor and jumped in the shower. I allowed the hot water to massage the back of my neck and flow down all over me. I closed my eyes and took a deep breath. Turned around and allowed the water to drench my entire body, the water flowed down my breast and I could feel my nipples become hard. I thought about my encounter with Bradd & briefly thought… Could it be fate that we crossed each other's paths tonight? Maybe… who knows… I grabbed my bullet, placed it on my naturally wet place and began pleasuring myself. It had been a while since I had been with a man. My ex and I weren't sexually compatible & I always knew that I needed someone more sexually experienced. It's not good to be deprived of what you need especially if you love sex. I glided the bullet up and down stimulating my clitoris and began to moan with satisfaction. I could feel myself tensing and trying to refrain from the climax as long as I could until I reached orgasmic haven and moaned "Ah ah ah ah, Aaahhhhhh, aaahhhhhh ummmmmmmm." Feeling my own juices flow down my inner thigh… I was finally ready for bed.

Chapter Two

October 27, 2015 10:37AM

Sitting in my office scanning in documents from the prior days cases, I heard a knock at my door. "Yes come in." I said.

"Good Morning baby!" It was my good friend and co-worker Alexis. People down south always called everyone either baby, sugar or sweetheart. Alexis was standing in my office door & wanted to inform me that they were holding a United Way rally and asked if I would like to bring in items for the bake sale.

"Of course." "You know I will help in any way I can. I think I'll make a five flavor pound cake."

"Great, thanks so much!"

"No problem girly."

"Hey, what did you bring for lunch?"

"I was rushing this morning and didn't have time to make my lunch…. Wanna do Pizza Wing King off of West Fairfield road?"

"Sure, I'll drive. Meet you outside at 12:45."

"Ok." I answered.

Right after she closed the door my office phone began to ring.

"Hello" I answered.

"Yes, this is Sidal from Sprint, just wanted to let you know that your phone has arrived, when would you like to pick it up?" The new phones were on backorder and just receiving this phone call made my day! "Yes Sidal, I will be in after work." He informed me that he wouldn't be there, but someone else would be able to assist me when I came in. I thanked him for his phone call and gently placed the phone back on the receiver. Five o'clock could not get here fast enough. Briefly thinking about my last moments in the store and how intense they were, I turned and looked out of my office window. It was a beautiful sunny day with just a few clouds in the sky. Three River Birch trees aligned the building across from my window and they swayed relaxingly in the breeze. I watched a few men move furniture from a warehouse to their truck. The name of the company was Liberty Furniture Industries right off of East Russell Avenue, in High Point. I worked in the heart of downtown, which was known as the furniture market capital of the world. They had some of the most beautiful wooden furniture anyone could ever want. If I could afford their furniture I would have a piece in every room. That's what quality will do; make you want all that it has to offer. That also goes for people, whenever I make true friendships I always look for the quality in a person.

We pulled up to the restaurant about fifteen minutes after leaving work. It didn't really take long to get there. We walked in and waited to be seated. This place has the absolute best wings in High Point. A slim Caucasian lady with long brunette hair greeted us and showed us to our booth.

"What can I get you two to drink? The waitress asked.

"I'll have a water with lemon." I responded.

"Water no lemon," said Alexis. "Oh and we know what we want to order." "I'd like the Jamaican wing dinner with French fries."

"I think I will get the honey barbeque wing dinner with a garden salad. House dressing please."

"Okie dokie, I will have your food out shortly." Hurriedly said the waitress.

"Ok Paris, so what's been going on with you lately? I realize its' been a while since you and Jasper separated. How are you adapting?"

"Honestly Alexis, I have to smile to keep from crying. There are times when I want to give up but I think about my kids and they are my motivation. I've totally devoted my time to work, taking on extra cases and working overtime just to keep my mind off of him." "Sometimes I think it's the only way I can keep my sanity." "Most marriages are salvageable however when you are straight and you find out your partner is gay there really isn't any way to salvage it & on top of that being looked up to by so many members at our church." "The thought that replays over and over in my head is... Paris, were there not any signs you ignored previously." I always try to blame myself for not picking up on it and trusting my intuition in the beginning of the relationship." "Even though I asked him if he was gay when we first started dating & he told me no, I should have trusted my intuition."

"Here you go ladies, Jamaican wing dinner with fries, & honey barbeque wing dinner with a salad." "Let me know if I can get you two anything else."

"Thank you," We both answered.

"Paris… its ok. We all have things that we regret in life. The most important thing is that no regret should outweigh the other." Said Alexis.

"All mistakes are mistakes, all sins are sins, no one should make you feel so bad that you can't make it and proceed with life."

"That is very true, however I find it hard to trust people now because of what I've been through."

I sighed, and then looked up at Alexis. She walked over, sat beside me gave me a big hug, looked me in the eyes and said,

"Everything is gonna be ok."
I really need to hear that. Thank you so much. We finished eating our lunch and hurried back to the office. I was scheduled for an 2 o'clock appointment and it was already 1:50pm.

I made it back to the office in just the nick of time. After assisting my last appointment, I glanced up at the clouds; I always had an interesting connection with nature. I found it to be a great stress reliever. I took a few deep breaths, crossed my legs and continued working on one of my cases. This client really needed my services and I was going to do everything in my power to help them. As I listened to the cars wisp by my window I glanced down at my watch. It was 4:55pm… I had been waiting for almost two weeks for this phone. Let me go ahead and clock out so I can pick my kids up and head to the store.

I pulled in the parking space right in front of the Noodles & Company restaurant, which was right beside the Sprint store. I looked up into my rear view mirror, made eye contact with my kids and said, "Alright, now when we get in here do not touch anything and try to be on your best behavior." Both Sammy & Simone snickered then answered, "Yes ma'am." I'm not quite sure why my heart is beating so fast... Could I be nervous at possibly seeing Bradd again? I thought, "Alright girl, get ahold of yourself!" I walked in the store and I immediately made eye contact with Bradd. I glanced away. He was standing in the back assisting another customer and somehow saw me come into the store. A female associate greeted me and asked how could she help me.

"I'm actually here to pick up my phone and get service started. I received a phone call from Sidal earlier today." I told her. She ensured me that someone would be with me as quickly as possible. My kids had found their way to the tablet section and began playing on them. I walked around the store and found the cutest pink and gold Katy Spade case. "Oh, I've got to have this." I said out loud.

"Mrs. James,"

I looked up and my eyes met those of Bradd's. "Good evening," I said. Keeping eye contact with him was hard to do. He was very handsome. He had a fresh shape up and his salt and pepper beard was full and straight. Facial hair was definitely my weakness. His eyes were light brown & were set close together paired with very full eyebrows. His fitted shirt graciously showed his muscular build.

"How are you?"

"I'm great, I'm just excited to finally be receiving my phone."

"You look absolutely amazing Mrs. James."

"Thank you Bradd,"

"My apologies that the phone took longer than expected. They are very popular and have been on backorder for a while."

"No problem, I understand."

"How are your kids, he glanced over at Sammy & Simone, I see they are growing well."

"Yes, they are keeping me busy. I have three now."

"So how is married life treating you?"

I glanced down and answered. "Not well actually, we aren't together anymore." I glanced back up; his eyes met mine.

"I'm sorry to hear that Mrs. James."

He continued assisting me with setting up my service. Once he was done he placed a glass protector on my phone.

"You are all set Mrs. James." He said as he smiled and handed me my phone. "Thank you very much for all of your assistance." I said. He reached for my hand, covered both of his hands over mine and said "Call me if you need anything."

Chapter Three

March 18, 2014 7:15AM

"Paris, I have some things I need to attend to today so I probably will be home late." Said Jasper, as he walked out the door with our daughter Joii.

"Ok, I will see you when you get back, have a good…"

The door closed before I could finish my statement. I don't know how much longer I can take this, I thought to myself. I stood facing the door. Tears were rolling down my face; I tried to regain control and finish getting ready. Jasper was an Evangelist and Co-Pastor at our church. He had been preaching for about 3 years. I was very proud of what he had accomplished for the church but if only he put the same effort at home. I knew I'd probably be wishing for that for the rest of my life. Our family life was suffering badly and I was the only one to see that. My bestfriend asked me to go on a short vacation with her so I decided to take a few days off of work and tag along. Angie & I were both from a small town in North Carolina called Wadesboro. We had been best friends since the eighth grade. We were heading to the Outer Banks to get in some relaxation and girl time. I heard my children's school bus pull up outside. I ran to the door and yelled,

"Have a good day!" "I love you both."

"Love you too ma," they said and hopped on the bus. Jasper and I owned our home. It was our 4th year living here in Washington. We both moved here October 2010. We owned a quaint two story house with four bedrooms & three bathrooms in Upper Chevy Chase Washington, DC. right off of NW Stephenson Place. Our home was known as the "Lilac House." I fell in love with this house because of the large sunken family-room and its historical features. The family room was painted pale blue with white crown molding and shutters dressed all the windows. The main focal point was the floor to ceiling brick fireplace. My son Sammy loved to read so we hired a contractor to build bookshelf's on both sides of the fireplace, that way we could have a place to hold all of the books that he had collected. I am a visual person and I had picked a few interesting oil paintings by Leonid Afremov and Renate Dubose. Afremov's paintings are amazingly vibrant and always seemed to make my heart smile and give me hope that things can and will be better. One painting in particular called "Quiet Town" was absolutely breathtaking. It reminded me of how something can look so calm and peaceful from an outsider's viewpoint but one never really knows what happens behind closed doors. Dubose's paintings are culturally captivating. I had purchased the Elovephant painting from her, which I felt expressed refreshing energy. I placed this painting at the top of the staircase. We both had decided on a white sectional from Lazzaro Leather & accented it with blue and white patterned pillows. I had come to love what we had built together but something inside of me knew that I built this life with the wrong person. People always say, "I don't have any regrets in life." I know for a fact I have regrets in life that I wish I could go back and change, to make a better educated decision, however since that is not possible I choose to move forward with my head held high. Letting those mistakes push me to be a better person. Ring... ring...

"Hello" I answered.

"Hey gal, what are you up to this morning?"

Angie and I had planned on leaving for the Outer Banks on the 20th once she finished her twelve-hour shift. Angie was a city police officer for the Fifth District Station in Washington DC. She had been working with them for the past 5 years.

"I'm packing for this trip. It's going to be so nice to just have some girl time."

"Yasss. I cannot wait to get out of this uniform."

"It can't be that bad girl…"

"Oh its not too bad, just the long shifts."

"Ok, well I will see you later on today."

"Alright gal."

My stomach started to rumble. I had been packing and cleaning all morning and decided to go out soon and get lunch. I pulled up to Blacks Bar & Kitchen around 2pm. I figured I'd wait so the lunch crowd would die down… boy was I wrong. This place was pretty busy. Most of the tables outside were filled. "I love this place, it had such a eco-friendly feel and the absolute best wine display. I hadn't eaten all day and I had so much on my mind. The waiter walked up to my table,

"Good Afternoon, are you ready to place your order?"

"Yes, I'll have the champagne sangria, the Black's Flapjacks with three premium oysters.

"Great choice! Will someone be joining you today?

"No, just for me, thank you." I smiled.

"Let me know if I can get you anything."

I looked around the restaurant, "Its such a nice day, I wish I could have sat outside" I thought to myself. I turned my head towards the bar area and couldn't believe what I was witnessing. "Is that my husband at the bar with some guy?" They were sitting closely together in a booth... a little too close. The guy that he was having lunch with had make-up on and his face was laid; eyebrows arched, high lighting and blush, anyone could tell that he had put in some time doing his make-up. However he still dressed in masculine attire. He had his hand placed on my husbands arm. Lightly rubbing it I saw Jasper smile.

"Ma'am, here is your drink."

I gasped for air.

"Ma'am, are you ok?"

"Thank you, can I actually have my food to go. Is it possible that they can box it up in the kitchen and bring it out as soon as possible? I had an emergency come up and I need to leave like... now."

"That wouldn't be a problem. I will be right back with your food."

I pulled out my American Express Platinum card. "Can you go ahead and process the payment too."

"Yes ma'am' I hope everything is ok."

"Thank you." I said as the waiter rushed off to the back of the restaurant. I always had my suspicions of my husband. Shaking my head back and forth I looked down closed my eyes and began stimulating my temples. The waiter was back in no time.

"Here you go, Thank you for coming in today."

"Thanks, I stood up from my chair and headed to the door. When I finally made it outside I took in a deep breath looked up into the clear blue sky and said, "why me?"

March 21,2014 8:00pm

"You ready to go Angie?"

"Yes gal, I'm ready."

"Ok well I just finished placing my luggage in the trunk. I'll swing by your place within the next hour ok."

"Alright, I will see you soon."

I threw my cell phone in my purse and headed to the kitchen, grabbed a few grapes, cheese sticks and a few slices of salami. Pulled out a zip-lock back and tossed the items in.

"Mom."

"Yes Joii"

"Where are you going mom?"

"Remember, I told you that I would be going on a mini vacation with your Aunt Angie. I'll be back on Monday ok."

"I love you mom."

"I love you too Joii." I picked up my little red head and gave her the biggest hug and kiss that I could. I walked upstairs and down the hall to Sammy's room. Both Sammy and Simone were sitting on the floor playing their Xbox 360 gaming system.

"Sammy, Simone, I'm about to leave ok. Have you guys brushed your teeth?"

"Yes mom, I've already picked out my clothes for tomorrow too!" Said Sammy.

"Great, I'm so proud of you!" "Love ya Sammy bear." I said as I walked over to Sammy and kissed his cheek.

"I'm all ready for bed ma," said Simone.

"I've brushed my teeth, taken my bath and brushed my hair. See I even have my bonnet on."

"Yes, I see that you are ready." I bent over and kissed her forehead.

"Love ya Simone, I'll see ya on Monday."

"Love you too ma."

I walked down the stairs to the study where Jasper was. I peaked in and saw that he was preparing for his sermon on Sunday. Knock, knock, and knock.

"May I come in?"

"Sure." He said quietly. I opened the door and walked inside.

"I'm about to leave."

"Ok, I will see you Monday and close the door on your way out." He said. He didn't even look up to acknowledge me. I turned around walked out of the study and closed the door.

Chapter Four

Angie and I hit the road around nine o'clock. We decided to leave late so we could avoid traffic. I knew that it would probably take us about six hours to get there so we planned on splitting the driving. We both were going through a very rough patch in our relationships with our significant others. Angie and her boyfriend of almost nine years were about to decide to call it quits.

"Girl I had such a long day… I made five arrests due to people driving while impaired. Do you mind driving the entire way?"

"No problem Angie, I gotcha girl."
Angie fell asleep two hours into the drive. We arrived at our hotel around 3am the next morning. We checked into one of the most famous and well-known hotels in the area. "The Inn at Rodanthe." I pulled up into the driveway and

parked in front of the hotel so we could unload our bags. A very nice gentleman greeted us.

"Welcome, My name Jose, I hope you both enjoy your stay."

"Thank you," Said Angie, "I will just get my bags out of the trunk. Paris can you pop the trunk?"

"Sure." Angie stepped out of the car and walked towards the back of the car to the trunk. She began to lift up her luggage.

"Ma'am' I will be happy to get that for you." He walked to the back of the car. Looked into Angie eyes then said, "May I have the bags ma'am?" Angie was so use to taking charge in all situations that she had somehow forgotten how to let someone take care of her. Jose was of Puerto Rican decent, tall and had the cutest smile. He advised us that he would be taking our bags to our room. He also checked us into our room since we arrived so late.

"We serve breakfast, which is included in your stay, from 5am until 11:30am." Jose said as he handed us our room keys. We were so happy to be checking into our room. We both were exhausted from the days' events and the drive. We fell asleep as soon as our heads hit the pillows.

The next morning we were awaken by the smell of freshly scrambled eggs, pancakes, and sausage. I went and took a long shower, dressed and headed down stairs. Angie was already downstairs at the table.

"Hey Angie"

"Good Morning gal."

I walked over to the table and took a seat across from Angie. An older lady came and bought me a plate and said "Enjoy!"

"Wow this looks great. I am starved."

"Oh its delicious," said Angie. "Just wait until you taste the eggs. They are so fresh."

"I really needed this. It feels so good to have someone else take care of you for a change." "Hey wanna go to the beach later. I just want to relax and let go of everything while I am here." I said to Angie. "Sure girl." We continued to eat our food. In walked Jose,

"Good morning ladies," he looked directly at Angie and said, "Good morning Angie."

"Good morning Jose," Angie said as she smiled then looked over at me with a very puzzled expression.

After eating we decided to change into our bikinis so we could enjoy the beach. Angie had a cute white strapless bikini top with boy shorts; she definitely had the body for it. She was a little smaller than I and was in great shape. Her profession required her to stay in shape. I wore a pale green lace halter bikini top with a lace thong bottom. I had recently had a bikini wax done just so I could wear this and it fit perfectly. We both snapped a few pictures then made our way outside. "This place is so serene." I said while walking through the tall grass just before entering the beach. Angie and I had found a nice spot not too far from the Inn. Although it was a fairly cloudy day there was a nice breeze in the air. You could literally smell the freshness of the ocean. I watched the waves crash back and forth revealing seashells and starfish in the sand. Sitting on the beach I pressed my toes into the sand, laid back on my towel and closed my eyes. Angie was directly beside me sitting on her towel.

"Paris."

"Yeah, what's up girl?"

"I'm done."

"I know Angie." I looked over at Angie and tears were streaming down her face. Angie wasn't one to show her feelings often. She was a very strong, independent woman; we both were and were raised to be that way by our parents.

"Angie."

"Yeah."

"I'm done too."

I sat up grabbed my best friend and gave her the biggest hug. We sat there and cried together, consoling one another.

"There are signs, I try to ignore them." "He said he loved me and wanted to be with me." "I asked him when we first started dating if he could possibly be homosexual just because he had some feminine ways about him." "He said no." "I'm so confused and don't know what to think. I'm so heartbroken… My heart literally hurts daily." "I'm on anti depressants now and I've never had to take those before." "I have panic attacks all of the time but mostly on my way home and when I am home." "This marriage will literally be the death of me if I don't do something soon."

"Paris you know that isn't healthy, you are a smart woman and you deserve someone who is going to love you unconditionally."

"I know," I replied, "And so do you Angie."

"The problem that I am having is that he denies it every time." "Makes me feel like I am loosing my mind & going crazy but I know I'm not." I tossed my hands in the air and then began rubbing my temples. "I've actually caught him checking out other guys." It is so sickening because he is suppose to by my husband. A man that I can lean on, depend on, trust with my heart, I should be his Queen, but I cannot compete with a man." "I've prayed, and I've prayed and I've prayed and things just seem to get worse." This marriage isn't salvageable." "Honestly, I don't think I was ever in love with him unconditionally."

"Really Paris? You don't mean that do you?"

"Yes I do, I don't believe we really spent enough time in the dating phase, I wasn't able to learn about his ways." "We didn't live together before we were married." "I just feel that it was so rushed." "Of course I love him, care about him but I am not in love with all of him."

"Wow, that's deep." Said Angie. "So what is your definition of love?"

"Love is simple." I looked up into the sky and smiled. "True love is loving a person so deeply that you love everything about them despite their flaws. You wouldn't want to change them, you are in love with their physical and mental, and most of all you are willing to stick with them despite anything and everything they may face in life. I don't feel that and I've ever felt that before with anyone. I should have never said yes. I honestly think I was too young and hadn't been able to experience life, learn, and mature as an adult."

We both sat there in silence for the next couple of hours listening to the waves. It felt so good to release the hurt and pain within. The sun had finally peaked through the clouds and I heard Angie saying,

"Lets go get some lunch." Angie jumped up and extended her hand to me.

"Now that sounds good to me!" I leaned forward, grabbed her hand and stood up; the sand had somehow made its way on to my legs, thighs & booty. I bent over to brush the sand off. Angie assisted me.

"Gal this sand isn't going anywhere. There is an outside shower near the inn. We can rinse off there."

"Ok great."

We headed back to our room to shower and get dressed to go out to lunch.

The next day was very pleasant. Angie and I were able to get some much-needed rest and we were now ready for an afternoon of shopping. I had packed the cutest strapless burnt orange jumper and paired it with some nice lace up sandals.

"Angie are you ready?"

"Yes I will be heading down in about five minutes, I just need to finish curling my hair."

"Ok, well I'm going to pull the car around. Are you going to drive?"

"Sure, I'll drive."

"Ok."

I headed downstairs. We were staying on the top floor. Our main reason for picking this particular hotel was that it has been known for mending relationships and represented a second chance on finding love. It also featured very nice balconies and an ocean front view from all bedrooms. I pulled the car around just as Angie was heading outside. I jumped out and ran over to the passenger's side. Angie jumped into the drivers seat.

"Where to?"

"Lets just drive until we see someplace interesting." Hatteras Island was such a beautiful place. It portrayed such an effervescent atmosphere. There was such beauty in the underdeveloped beach areas. I actually want to visit some of the local spots, mom and pop restaurants and small businesses. Once we hit the road we came upon a little cape cod two-story shop called Island Spice & Wine. "Lets stop here Angie," I said. Angie pulled in and parked the car. I am a wine connoisseur so was very interested to see what they had to offer. When we walked in we could see that they had a variety of products, including gifts, coffee, food and other liquors. I came across a bottle of Vision Cellars 2010 Rosella's Vineyard & Garys' Vineyard Santa Lucia Highlands Pinot Noir. I purchased both bottles and couldn't wait to get them home and pop them open. Angie came across some of Dave's Insanity

Gourmet Spices. She loved making Mexican food. She actually made this Taco Bake that was to die for and I'm sure these spices would kick it up a notch. We made our purchases and continued our drive. Right when we pulled up to the Tanger Outlet in Nags Head she received a phone call. I picked my phone up out of my purse… No calls or text from Jasper. I sighed.

"Paris," said Angie. "We are going to have to cut our little vacation a day short."

"Noooo, why, what's going on?" I said disappointingly.

"That was my boss, I've been assigned a case that needs attention now." "I reminded him that I was on vacation so he advised me that I would have to report to work tomorrow at 6am." "I'm so sorry Paris."

"Ok, I understand. What time do you need to be on the road?"

"I'm thinking around six o'clock this evening that way I will be able to sleep a few hours before work."

"Ok, that's cool. I'll drive back since I have the next few days off, I will be able to get ample rest."

"Thanks so much bestie!" Angie said as she smiled.

"I'll call the Inn and let them know we have to check out early."

"Great, lets run in here really quick and find some deals."

We grabbed our purses and shopped for a couple of hours then headed back to the Inn.

When we arrived at our room all of our bags were packed.

"Wow, what great service!"

Knock... knock... knock... Angie scurried to the door.

"Who is it?"

"It's Jose." Angie turned around looked at me and shrugged her shoulders then opened the door.

"I hope you all enjoyed your stay."

"Yes Jose, we did. Thank you for all of your hospitality."

"No problem, I will be happy to take your luggage to your car for you."

"Thank you, we would appreciate that greatly." Jose carried the luggage down to the car while we checked out of our room. When we arrived to our car we snapped one more picture together then I jumped into the drivers seat. As Angie walked over to the passenger's side Jose stopped her and said.

"Angie, it was a pleasure meeting you."

"Likewise Jose, thanks for being so nice to us both."

"Angie I don't mean to pry but I think you are a very attractive woman and I would love to get to know you more."

"Jose, things are complicated right now."

"I understand," Jose said as he turned to walk away.

"How about you give me your number and I will contact you when things calm down." Angie said.

"Great!" Jose said as he took down Angie's phone number.

Chapter Five

November 4, 2015

I noticed my phone blinking. I must have received a message... I picked up my cell phone. It was from Bradd. He had contacted me via Facebook messenger.

"Hello Mrs. James."

"Hi Bradd. How are you?"

"Are you busy?"

"No, not right now, just studying French. Corny right. I normally spend my free time studying."

"No, Absolutely not. I've been thinking about you."

"Its good to hear from you Bradd."

"Are you enjoying your phone?"

"Oh, Yes I love my phone. Its amazing."

"That's good to hear." "Mrs. James I'd love to hang out with you, take you to dinner or lunch one day."

Looking down at my phone I thought of all the things I could say to avoid this date, it had been a while since I'd actually been on a date. However I was also mutually interested in Bradd as he was in me.

"That would be nice." I answered. "I don't get much free time but we could do lunch November 12th. I'm working a half-day that day." I said as I checked my calendar.

"Ok Mrs. James, November 12th. Enjoy your evening. I look forward to seeing you again."

The Unknown

Gazing into the blankness of the atmosphere

Leary of what could be, the unknown is so stimulating

Stimulating the mind, body, soul

Taking another chance

What could be could be forever

What could be could last a moment

What could be could be

Feeling the particles of peacefulness flow into me

A calmness soothing my soul

Giving hope and faith to the unknown

The unknown could be so captivating

The unknown could be so questionable

The unknown could be so leery

However with out experiencing the unknown

You will never know what could have been

Experience freely

Take another chance

Chapter Six

March 24, 2014

I finally arrived home around 1am, a lot earlier than expected. I didn't want to be loud since it was so early in the morning. I knew the kids and my husband would be sleeping. I didn't tell Jasper that I would be home early so I knew he wouldn't be expecting me and I didn't want to startle him. I inserted my key and turned the lock. The door opened. "Ok, he didn't lock the top chain… so I don't have to go around to the back door." I said to myself. I walked in and kicked my shoes off, sat my purse down on the side table, turned around to close and lock the door, which creaked a little but wasn't loud enough to wake anyone. There was a staircase right off of the entrance of our home leading upstairs to the bedrooms. "I'm so tired," I thought to myself. My hair had been pulled into a messy high ponytail all day. I pulled the band out and shook my head to loosen up my hair. I ran my fingers through my hair until it fell in place. I placed one foot on the first step to head upstairs so I could get some much-needed sleep. As I started to head upstairs I realized that I wouldn't be able to sleep without getting some water first. My mouth was very dry and I always drink at least a glass of water before bed. I turned around and headed to the kitchen. As I walked though the foyer and through the family room I looked over at our sectional couch in the family room...

"What the Fuck is going on?" I screamed. I saw Jasper and some guy spooning and sleeping together on the couch. I was so startled by what I saw that I fell back onto the hardwood floor as if someone had literally pushed me down. I scurried up and stumbled to the light switch, turned it on. They were both naked.

"David, from church?" "What the Fuckkkkkkkkk?" David was Jasper's right hand man. He and Jasper were always together doing the work of the Lord, so I thought.

"Somebody better start talking and I mean NOW!"

"It's not what it appears to be Paris." Said Jasper

"Are you sleeping with him?"

"No, we are just friends but we have never crossed that line."

"But I'm sure you've thought about it." Jasper lowered his head in shame he answered,

"Yes."

"Oh my God! What the fuck?"

"Why are you cursing?"

"Don't tell me what the fuck to do! I'm done!"

"No you aren't."

"Do you expect me to stay in this marriage? You like men."

"Yes I expect you to stay in it. Everyone at church knows us as the power couple, we inspire so many people."

"It's a lie!" "& I cannot live a lie for the rest of my life."

"He is my confidant Paris."

"I'm suppose to be your confidant Jasper!" Jasper approached me, I pushed him away, he looked around and found his shorts, tugged them on. David stood back in the corner like a little Bitch.

"Get the fuck out!!!"

"No, I'm not going anywhere & he isn't either," Jasper said. My heart was beating so fast, I could literally feel the hairs on my arms stand up, anger was boiling from within, my skin flushed red, my left eye started to twitch, with tears streaming down my face I somehow regained control of myself, my emotions, my anger. My body had been stimulated by so many feelings and emotions that I no longer felt a connection with planet earth.

"So this is what you want?" I said.

"Paris you are blowing this way out of proportion."

"You are sleep on the couch completely naked with another man!" Jasper you know I don't have anything against gay people but when it involves my marriage I do." "You know why?" "Because I'm not gay, I'm not bi-sexual." "If you are gay you need to fully accept it because you aren't doing anything but hurting me and hurting yourself." "I asked you when we first started dating if you could possibly be gay and you know what you said to me?" "You said No!" "You lied Jasper, you lied!" I started to sob. I walked upstairs, looked over the balcony and saw that David and Jasper were getting dressed. I walked into my bedroom and climbed into the bed. I heard the Jasper and David begin to argue, and then the front door slammed closed. My heart had broken into a thousand pieces. I always knew the definition of sobbing however I never experienced it until that day. I sobbed until morning.

March 24,2014

I woke up around 6:00am to wake the kids and ensure they had enough time to get ready for school. I realized that I still had my clothes on from the prior day. I went downstairs to make a quick breakfast, scrambled eggs and toast. I noticed that Jasper wasn't home. I made the kids plates and headed back upstairs to shower and get ready for work. I walked into the bathroom, looked up in the mirror; my eyes along with the bags under my eyes were extremely swollen. I couldn't stop the tears from streaming down my face. I looked like complete and utter shit. My heart had just been crushed into a million pieces and my husband didn't even care. I turned on the shower, stepped in and just stood there. I imagined the water washing away all of my problems, mistakes, failures, and disappointments. I though about all of the good times Jasper & I had and if they could possibly outweigh the bad. Nothing could outweigh this feeling and I instantly knew what the end result would be. I hated myself for being so naive and committing to someone who wasn't able to love me. After about twenty minutes in the shower I stepped out and smoothed baby oil all over my body, looked at myself in the mirror, the puffiness was still there. "Well Paris you've got to pull this off today," I said to myself. I was facilitating a meeting at work and had put so much time into the prep work and the prospective clients that no matter what was going on in my personal life it was going to have to take a backseat to my career. I never really knew the true meaning of separating work from personal life until this very day.

After I perfected my make up and hair I looked in the closet adjacent to the bathroom. We had a very large walk in closet. My things aligned one side and Jaspers the other. I pulled out my favorite suit. It was a flared white and black peppercorn blazer with an a line knee length pencil skirt & a white blouse. I decided to pair it with some cute but professional black fishnet stockings and black pumps. As I made my way downstairs I shouted,

"Alright kids its time to go, are you ready?" The kids were sitting at the table finishing up their breakfast. They did a pretty good job of getting ready without me having to remind them constantly to do certain things. I brushed up my little girl's hair and we headed out the door.

Chapter Seven

Survival

Gasping for air

Reaching for a thread

Searching for hope

One comes into this world

Knowing in this life you are alone,

One must learn to love ones' self

Knowledge of true happiness and contentment is required

You're all you've got.

Gasping for air

Reaching for a thread

Searching for hope

One continues in this world

Discernment is learned

The hardest moments in your life enlighten your senses

Enable you to question rituals, religions & traditions.

Forcing growth or death

Trusting your internal intuition can prevent the

Internal crushing of your being

Life's terrain is full of hills, mountains,

Slopes & plateaus however its your choice to continue

Gasping for air

Reaching for a thread

Searching for hope

One is educated in this world

Knowing in this life you can make it

One day, one minute, one hour, one moment at a time

You can prevent the Internal crushing of your being

And you can choose to Survive.

Chapter Eight

November 12, 2015

What a day… As I walked out of my office the only thing going through my mind was how fast I could get to my car. Deeply anticipating my date with Bradd yet hadn't held a real conversation with in some time. It seemed like every time I called him my call would go to voicemail. Sigh… "Ok Paris, you can do this," I said to myself. Trying to pep myself up since I hadn't been on a date in a while. Being separated yet still married is kind-a hard to explain but nevertheless he asked and I agreed. It was a pretty nice warm day for November, the sun was shining and there was a very crisp breeze in the air. I pulled up at TGI Friday's in Greensboro, right off of Wendover and waited inside. There were two bubbly greeters who greeted me with a smile and asked if I was waiting on someone. As I began to reply I felt a hand on the small of my back.

"Bradd, how are you?" I turned and greeted him with a hug. He looked very nice, was dressed in a dark brown leather jacket, a cute brown & red hat from Old Navy paired with nice antique blue jeans. It had been a while since I had been in the presence of another man and he definitely was masculine enough for me, considering what my ex had to offer. "Stop thinking about your ex," I said to myself over and over again. The hostess guided us to our booth near the front of the restaurant. We sat down and started to chat. Bradd looked up and into my eyes, then looked away.

"You are beautiful. You're eyes are gorgeous."

"Thank you," I said blushingly.

I've been told before that I have hypnotizing eyes. They are almond shaped, light green & very seductive. I suppose they were a perfect match for my coke bottle figure, chocolate skin and natural wavy hair. Bradd didn't make much eye contact however the conversation was pleasant and we both enjoyed being with the other. One thing I noticed is Bradd's phone kept ringing but he would ignore the call.

"Do you need to answer your phone?"

"Nope." I nodded my head. I ordered the Jack Daniels shrimp & chicken; my absolute favorite and he ordered a plate of hot wings with fries. I studied his face;

he looked as if he had been through a hurtful past relationship. As we talked about my past and his, I found it to be exciting to see where this could possibly go despite the fact I had given up on love, trust, and commitment in a relationship. I always try to remind myself that life is like a deck of cards, no matter what hand you are dealt play it well. It's your life and there is no right or wrong way to live it. The waitress brought our food to the table; which smelled absolutely delightful. Bradd reached for a wing.

"Are you going to say the grace?" I asked.

"Who me?" said Bradd.

"Yes." I stretched my arms on the table and opened up my hands, he grabbed my hands, held them tight and said,

"Can you pray this time? I'm not too good at this type of thing."

"Of Course." I said, and then I led the prayer. We began to eat our food.

"Mrs. James, how are your kids doing?"

"They are doing great despite the separation. They are so smart and have excellent grades in school." Bradd nodded and said. "That's Amazing!"

"So Bradd, how long have you been single?"

"I've been single for about a year. My ex and I dated

for about three years and I just didn't see myself marrying her or having children with her. It was hard moving on after being with someone for so long but I'm ready to move on now. So what exactly happened between you and your ex?"

I took a deep breath, looked directly at Bradd. My eyes began to tear up.

"We don't have to talk about that right now."

"Ok."

"Do you think you are ready for another relationship? I mean are you emotionally stable considering everything you have been through?"

I thought for a minute...

"I believe that I am ready for love. I'm ready for a relationship. I'm not saying that I have fully recovered and healed from the hurt but I am ready to move forward, no looking back. You know everything we experience in life, leaves an everlasting print in your heart. Its up to you to decide mentally what to do with that experience."

"True. So do you feel that the marriage could have been saved?"

"In all honesty... No, the marriage was not salvageable."

We finished our meal and he walked me to my car.

"Thank you for having dinner with me Mrs. James."

"Thank you for inviting me Bradd."

He stretched his arms out. I walked up to him and gave him a very light hug.

"Aw man… I get the church hug with the pat on the back. Really… I'm going to have to teach you how to hug."

I laughed and gazed into his eyes. He leaned in and kissed me on my forehead and wrapped his arms around me. It felt so good to be embraced this way.

"Have a good evening Ms. James," Bradd said, then opened my car door. I got in and cranked my car up, he leaned in and kissed me on the cheek, closed my door then walked to his Jeep. Wow, what an awesome date, I thought. I looked down at my watch. Oh my, where did the time go?

I headed to my mother's house. I had agreed to drive my aunt Macie, who had been staying with my mother for about a month, to Atlanta this evening. She was scheduled to have surgery at Atlanta's Northside Hospital the following Friday morning. I pulled into my mother's driveway sat in my car for a few, just to get myself together to deal with mommy dearest. I stepped out of my white BMW M4 Gran Coup that had an all white leather interior, tinted windows, sunroof and the best system you could ever wish for. I had always loved music and found it to be an outlet for me, so I have to go all in when it comes to what I love.

"Hi mom," I said, as I entered the living room. My mother is such a traditional Christian lady. She loves to hang pictures on her walls, showcase her fine china in her beautiful china cabinet, and talk about the goodness of the Lord. As I took a seat I asked my Aunt Macie if she was ready for the ride to Atlanta. She answered,

"I guess so."

"Good! Are you ready for the surgery? I mean are you ready mentally?"

"I think so, I've wanted and needed this surgery for quite some time now."

We started to load the car so we could head out around 8pm. I had worked a half a day and was very tired however I wanted to help my aunt out as much as I could. Also I had never been to Atlanta and was looking forward to the trip. I had a few friends that moved there and I was excited to see them again.

After an extremely tiring drive we finally pulled up into the hotel around 2:00am. OMG… That was the longest drive of my life since I did all of the driving. We checked into the hotel just so we could catch a couple hours of sleep. Ding… Ding… Ding… was the sound of the alarm at six o'clock that morning.

"I swear to you if feels like I just blinked." I said as I woke up.

"Dang… it's time to get up already?"

"Yes Aunt Macie. I'm going to lay here a little while longer while you go shower and get ready."

"Ok…"

I laid back down for just a few more minutes. Then decided to go ahead and get up. I was so exhausted from the long drive and hardly any sleep. Now it was time to drive Aunt Macie to the hospital for surgery.

Once Aunt Macie was headed back for surgery a nurse approached me and advised me that she would be in surgery for approximately 6 hours. She asked for my phone number in case of any emergencies. I gave her my phone number and headed outside to the car to try and get some more sleep. After a few hours past, I decided to grab something to eat. I started the engine and headed to Starbucks. I needed some strong coffee to get me through the day. I searched for the closest Starbucks in my Maps app. "Alright, here is one right off of Peachtree St NE." "It shouldn't take me but a few minutes to get here," I said to myself. As I drove to my destination I received a text message.

"Good morning Paris, It's me Zaron. I was wondering if you made it down. I recall you telling me you would be down in Atlanta this weekend. If you are let me know. Would love to see you. It's been too long."

I hadn't seen Zaron in over six years. We grew up together and were so close. After I came to a stop I quickly responded to his text.

"Hi Zaron, It's so good hearing from you. Yes I am down; my Aunt Macie is currently in surgery. I'm sure we will be in town for a few days, the Dr. probably won't release her to leave until Sunday."

Zaron replied,

"Great, call me whenever you are free. I will answer."

Zaron was a producer with a major record company in Atlanta, right at the corner of Northside Drive NW and Trabert Ave NW. He had been working there for a few years and was one of the best producers there. He was always super busy with work and didn't work the normal 8-5 so his hours were very different from the average Joe. I responded,

"Will do."

It was a surprisingly beautiful November day. Warm, sunny and breezy. I found a parking space a few blocks away and headed in for my tall flat macchiato with an extra shot of espresso. The line was very long however moved fairly quickly. I took a sip; the coffee was absolutely superb. "Ahhhh, so good." I whispered, as I took a seat outside at one of the unoccupied tables. I suddenly felt my phone vibrate and pulled it out of my pocket. It was the hospital calling. I answered.

"Hello, Mrs. James?"

"Yes this is Mrs. James."

"This is the head nurse calling from the Hospital, just wanted to inform you that Macie is out of surgery. We are moving her to the recovery room where she will be for the next couple of hours"

"Thank you, I will be back shortly."

Chapter Nine

May 25, 2014

Memorial Day.

I was very happy to be off of work. The kids were out of school, and I had planned to have a very nice cookout. Invited a few close friends of mine over since Jasper was attending a cookout with his friend David. Things between Jasper and I had worsened. There was no emotional connection, no love, no words of kindness, or anything positive. He forbid me to speak with the Bishop of our church and even my friends at the church. I've never known the feeling on being alone until I met Jasper. I've always been happy being alone as a single person but now it felt so different. Maybe I felt this way because I was still married to my husband yet no relationship. I often sat dazed and in silence. I had been prescribed Xanax from my Doctor just to keep my crying spells down and to a minimum. I reached for the Belvedere Vodka and poured a tall glass of it then added a splash of cranberry mango juice. I continued prepping the food for the cookout. I had a menu that included Caribbean Jerk chicken wings, bacon wrapped chicken, burgers, hot dogs, grilled corn & homemade potato salad. The jerk wings had been marinating for a couple of days so they would be very spicy. "Ding dong," the doorbell rang. It was my good friend Angie and a few other friends from my church. I was a little tipsy, however considering the current situation I really didn't give a damn.

"Please come in. Make yourselves at home." I said as I walked my friends in and to the family room. The kids were outside playing & I had turned on some nice music for us to vibe to.

"Where is Jasper?" asked the choir director from our church.

"Jasper is attending a different cookout with a close friend," I replied.

"That's just like Jasper, always doing the Lords work no matter what. I'm sure you probably wanted him here."

"Of course I do but I have come to accept having to sacrifice so much being a pastors wife." "Believe it or not

I'm often placed at the bottom of the list, along with the kids."

"My God, My God, Paris how do you deal with it?" asked sister Petree.

"I don't anymore," I answered. They all looked very puzzled. I picked up my phone, no missed calls or text. Poured me another cocktail and headed outside to start the grill up. Everyone was having such a wonderful time. The kids were outside in the back yard swinging and playing tag. My son Sammie was playing basketball with a few other kids in the neighborhood. I pulled the lid open and placed some charcoal on the grill. "Where is that lighter fluid?" I said out loud.

"Could it be in the storage building?" Said Angie.

"It could be, do you mind checking?"

"No problem," Angie said as she walked over to the storage building. The day had been so weird. Even though I was interacting with everyone I was still kind of in a dazed state. After all I had been emotionally & spiritually broken trying to live with the fact my husband was gay and move forward.

"I found it!" Shouted Angie.

"Great let me hold it so I can get this grill started so we all can eat." I shouted as I laughed. Angie tossed me the lighter fluid.

"Girl, I almost dropped it, hahaha"

"Girl I think you might need to slow down with the vodka."

"Look Angie I am fine Ok! Can you pass me the chicken wings and hamburger patties please?"

The food was ready within the hour. We all ate and had an amazing time, shared stories about our children, church and careers. Around 9:45pm almost everyone had left. Angie was still there with her daughter.

"Alright gal, I think we are about to head home. I've got to work in the morning and I've got to get my little one to school."

"Ok girl, come here." I gave Angie and her beautiful little girl a hug. "I will see you both very soon ok. Oh and Angie I haven't forgot about Jose." Angie smiled and said,

"See ya gal. Love ya."

"Love you too Angie." I said, Angie could see that I was hurting deep within.

"You can get past this Paris, you are strong. Let me know if you need me."

Everyone had left. The kids were taking their baths and preparing for bed. I looked up at the clock in the foyer, it was about 10:25pm and Jasper still hadn't made it home. I started to dwell on what had happened between Jasper and I the past couple of months. I walked to the kitchen and poured another tall glass of vodka on the rocks. Looked in the sink; which was full of dishes. Angie did offer to stay and help me clean up but my emotional stated needed privacy. "Let me check on the kids," I said to myself. I walked upstairs. The kids had bathed and changed into their pj's. They were actually in bed... I laughed to myself and said, "They must have played hard today." I gave them all a kiss and tucked them in.

I walked back downstairs and made my way outside. The grill was still hot. I pulled the grill out from beside the house until it was in the middle of the backyard and threw a few more charcoals on it. Doused it in lighter fluid then threw a match onto it. The blaze was so high and bright as if it was filled with pure hatred and anger. After taking a few sips of my drink I headed upstairs to our bedroom, opened the door to Jaspers closet, grabbed a handful of suits still on the hangers, tossed them over one arm, grabbed a few pairs of dress shoes in the other and headed back downstairs out the backyard. Staring at the blazing fire I threw them into the grill, the last scene replaying over and over in my mind was finding Jasper and David sleeping together in our family room. I ran into the kitchen, picked up the bottle of Belvedere and just turned it up, trying to kill the pain inside. I stumbled upstairs and repeated the process until every last piece of him was gone. I found a couple of cufflinks on the dresser, grabbed them and once I made my way outside I threw them onto the fiery blaze. The air smelled of rubber, burnt plastic, chemicals and pure evil. It was such a foul odor, just as foul as Jasper had been towards our family. I took a few steps back, looked into the blaze and allowed all of the hurt and pain burn away, then gazed up into the starry night, lifted my arms into the air and screamed

"Why me God! Why me?" I fell to my knees, tears rolling down my face, I lay in the grass in the fetal position crying.

When I woke up I was still outside, I must have been out for a couple of hours. I managed to muster up the strength to get up and walk inside. I stumbled through the back door, made my way through the family room upstairs to the bathroom. Kneeled down to turn on the water, ran a hot bath. Tugged off my clothes very sloppily and got in. That night I did a large amount of thinking, I felt so weak. Jasper never made it home that night.

Chapter Ten

November 13, 2015

I arrived back at the hospital around 2pm. Aunt Macie had been moved from the recovery room and had been admitted into a hospital bed. I walked up to the nurse's station.

"Excuse me, can you tell me which room Macie Jones has been moved into?" A nurse stood up, looked at me and said,

"Are you Paris, the lady I called a few hours ago?"

"Yes, that's me."

"She has been moved to room 344, it's not too far from here.

Ok, thank you!" I replied as I made my way down the hall. I arrived at Aunt Macie's room and slowly opened the door. She was sleeping. I walked in and around her bed, placed my items in the closet and sat down in the reclining chair.

"Paris," Aunt Macie whispered.

"Hey, how are you feeling?" I asked as I walked over to her and rubbed her forehead.

"I'm feeling ok, still very sore."

"I can imagine, just take it slow. I think they are giving you pain medication and they will be bringing you something to eat soon."

"Ok, I'm very thirsty. Can you get me some ice?"

"Sure," I looked over at my phone and saw that it was blinking. Grabbed it up and went to get some ice. I glanced down at my phone; I had received a text from my friend Zaron.

Hey Paris, if you are free later on tonight meet me at the studio around 10pm, then we can go out later. I'll send you the address.

After ensuring that my aunt had everything she needed I jumped in the shower and got dressed to go see Zaron. It was a cold dark night. I had decided to wear some black jeans with a dark green sweater and paired it with some Gucci fur boots. It only took me about twenty minutes to arrive at his studio. When I pulled up it actually looked like an abandoned building. It was fenced in with a large gate on the entrance. I called Zaron to let him know I had arrived, the gate swung open and I pulled up and into a parking spot. As I turned my car off, Zaron walked out the door. I stepped out of the car.

"Zaron, how are you its been forever since I've seen you." Zaron was a about my height and slim, he had a close fade with a closely shaved beard and mustache. He was biracial, African American & Caucasian. Very light skinned with light grey eyes. He was dressed very nicely, had a button up white dress shirt with a black skinny tie, black Yeezy pants and some all white Adidas. He looked very sharp.

"Its been too long Paris," Zaron said as he gave me a hug.

"It's cold out here, come in." Zaron grabbed my hand and led me inside. Gave me a tour of the studio, which was super dope! Zaron was a great producer and made the some of the best music and worked with well-known artist. He took me to his studio and played a few beats for me.

"I am so happy for you, you're doing what you love and that is a blessing." I said as I listened to a song that he wrote about me. Zaron and I had history, we dated years ago before I had children and always kept in contact with one another.

"Are you ready to go, have you had dinner?"

"No I've been at the hospital all day, I'm very hungry."

"I know a place we can go, eat, dance, have fun, just talk and catch up."

"That sounds nice."

He led me back outside and told me to wait while he pulled his car around. As I waited my phone vibrated, it was Bradd. He had sent a text message.

"Hello dear, call me when you are free."

It was just something about this guy that I really liked. I tried to call him but no answer. I shook my head. It had been very hard getting him on the phone and holding a conversation with him. I can remember the first time we met, we were both working for a prestigious bank in the mortgage department. I was just engaged to Jasper the day before he approached me to ask me for my phone number. Once he saw the ring on my hand he apologized and said he didn't know I was taken, I told him I was just engaged the evening before. He grasped his hands together and took a deep breath before walking back to his office. At that very moment I wondered if I was making a mistake by saying yes to Jasper. Not because I was attracted to Bradd but because I didn't truly know if I loved Jasper. Bradd & I also had a few other encounters at the gym. We would talk briefly; I would always notice him looking at my hand to see if I still wore my wedding ring. I am one that believes in love at first sight. Some people are blessed to experience it and others aren't. I left a voicemail for Bradd with hopes that he would eventually call me back.

Zaron pulled up in an all white BMW i8 Coupe, I jumped in and we headed out.

"So where are we going?" I said as he sped down the road.

"I'm going to take you to this place called Ormsby's. It's a bar, restaurant and hangout spot all in one. The food is delicious. I think you will like it."

"Alright, sounds good to me."

Zaron pulled into a parking deck and we walked a short distance until we arrived at Ormsby's. The place was decked out. Zaron gave them his name since there was a short wait for a table. We found a table in the bar area.

"What would you like to drink?"

"Ummm, think I'll have a mojito."

"I'll be back," Zaron walked off to the bar to order our drinks. I called Aunt Macie but she didn't answer. She's probably sleeping, I thought to myself. Zaron arrived back at the table with our drinks. We sat and talked about various topics, including my marriage, his relationship status, religion, spirituality, and science. We eventually made our way to a booth and ordered. The food was spectacular, I ordered the Cajun Roasted Chicken which came with Mac & cheese, rainbow swiss chard and red pepper veloute sauce, Zaron ordered the fresh Baja fish tacos.

"Zaron this place is Amazing, how did you find out about this spot."

"I met this guy who wanted me to produce an album for him and this is the spot he wanted to meet at. I've been coming here ever since." Zaron said, I nodded my head and continued eating my entree.

"Paris, you deserve so much better." He stared straight into my eyes.

"I don't know what I did to deserve this." I said as I rubbed my temples. Zaron walked over to where I was sitting slid in the booth and placed his arms around me and said,

"You deserve so much more." He leaned in for a kiss, I leaned forward then backed away.

"I can't Zaron, I'm dating someone." Looking into his eyes, he turned away and said,

"Is it serious Paris?"

"No not yet, we are in the early stages but I am interest in the possibility of what could be." Zaron looked down at me in disappointment.

"I'm always here for you Paris."

"Paris, do you need a place to stay tonight? I know that recliner at the hospital is not comfortable."

"I think I'll be fine." Zaron took my hand and said,

"Paris, you are staying with me tonight, it's the least I could do for you." I nodded my head in agreement. We finished our meal and headed back to his place.

Chapter Eleven

November 14, 2015 Atlanta, GA 1:22AM

As Zaron sped down the highway he looked over at me & took my hand in his. I glanced up to see where we were headed. We took Tech Parkway NW to HWY 8 before we turned left onto Oakdale Rd. I saw a sign that read welcome to Druid Hills. The streets were well lit and I could see that every yard was well landscaped. After about a mile we pulled into the driveway. Zaron owned a very large tri level majestic brick home with lovely columns that aligned the entrance. He pressed the garage door opener in his car and we pulled in.

"This is home." Zaron stated as he opened his door and walked over to mine. "Watch your step babe." Zaron took my hand and helped me out.

"Thank you." I looked up at Zaron.

"Paris you deserve so much better I want to give that to you." Zaron led me into his home.

"Wow, this is nice Zaron."

"Thank you, it took a lot of tiring days and extremely long hours of working non stop."

"I can imagine! I know every time we seem to talk on the phone or even text you are working."

"Yes, that's the norm for me. That's why I have yet to get into a relationship with anyone. I just didn't have the time to put into one."

I looked up at Zaron and nodded my head in understanding.

"Paris I want to ask you a question."

"Ok, shoot."

"This guy Bradd, that you are friends with. Does he show you that he is interested?" "I don't mean to pry but if you were my woman I would be calling you, checking on you especially if you were out of town to see if you were ok or even it you needed anything of me." I took a few moments to think as I followed Zaron into his home. We walked through a spectacular kitchen and living room and finally arrived in the sunroom. The sunroom was lined with floor to celling windows; I could just imagine how beautiful the room would be during the day.

"Have a seat, would you like something to drink?"

"Sure." I smiled. As Zaron walked off he said,

"I'll be right back sweetheart. Make yourself at home, feel free to look around, I'm going to make us a couple of drinks and grab few snacks from the fridge."

"Ok," I stated as I stood up from the lounge chair and began to explore a little, I was also still pondering his prior question. I did like Bradd, but did he like me just as much? After giving it some thought it was pretty clear that he didn't. He was only interested in the occasional "hang out" but nothing more.

I found the entrance to the home that embraced a lovely foyer that had the most marvelous marble floors I've ever seen.

"Paris"

I glanced over to look at him. He walked towards me and said, " Lets sit and talk, oh and I have snacks."

"What kind of snacks do you have?" I veered my head down and looked up questionably squinting my eyes.

"Well… I have Rock of Ages Bushy Fork Red wine, crackers & some aged cheddar cheese." Zaron said as he looked at me and shrugged his shoulders.

"That actually sounds really good. Oh and that is one of my favorite wines."

"Awesome! I actually need to go shopping. Wish you were going to be in town longer."

"I know but I can always plan a trip down & you know you are more than welcomed to come up my way." Zaron proceeded to pour me a glass of wine.

"Lets make a toast to new beginnings." Zaron said as he held his glass up.

"New beginnings!" I said as we toasted and drank the wine, which tasted absolutely superb. Our eyes met, he leaned in for a kiss. I met him this time and we shared a long hot exciting & loving kiss.

"I want you Paris but I know I can't have you right now but I am willing to wait until you figure everything out with your ex." "Come with me." Zaron said as he led me upstairs and into his master bedroom, which was fit for a king of course.

"You can sleep here tonight. I'll be right down the hall in the next bedroom. I think we need to call it a night." He wrapped his arms around me, kissed me on my forehead and said, "Sweet dreams pretty face." I looked up at him and smiled. He knew I loved when he called me that.

I walked over to the bed, sat down and looked around. The room was decorated in white, gold and navy blue. An ancient stone Hindu sculpture that sat on the chest along with a few sticks of bamboo in a tall vase. There was a bathroom adjacent from the bed. I walked in

and turned on the shower and thought to myself…
another lonely night. One thing I hated about being
separated was sleeping alone. I can say that when I was
married I enjoyed having someone there with me at night.
After I showered I walked to the bed, dropped my towel
and got under the covers. Before I knew it I was fast
asleep.

I opened my eyes and pulled my phone from the
nightstand. It was 9:18am. I must have been very tired.
"No missed calls from my aunt." I said to myself. I walked
into the bathroom and grabbed a robe. As I made my way
down the hall I peaked into the next bedroom, Zaron was
nowhere to be found. "Ok" I thought to myself, maybe he
went for a morning run. I do remember him telling me he
enjoys daily morning runs. I made my way downstairs and
into the kitchen. Zaron had made breakfast. There was a
covered plate on the bar along with a note, which read,

Enjoy your breakfast Luv. Be back shortly.
Zaron.

Zaron had made scrambled cheese eggs, buttered
grits and sautéed shrimp with a side of assorted fruit. The
plate was still warm so he couldn't have been gone long.
There was a fresh pot of coffee too. I had to indulge in my
simple pleasure. I poured a large cup and sipped. It was so
deep, dark, rich and bold. It was exactly what I needed.

Coffee seemed to sooth my pain, the pain of waking up every morning with regrets, pain of heartbreak, and pain of failure. One thing about persistence is that each day does get better than the day before however the pain and hurt never truly goes away. As I finished eating I heard the front door open.

"Its me Paris." Zaron said as he entered. He walked into the kitchen.

" How did you sleep?"

"I slept so peacefully, your bed is very comfortable."

"It should be for the amount of money I paid."
Zaron chuckle. "& Did you enjoy your breakfast?"

"Yes, I did. Thank you."

"Anything for you Paris. Have you heard anything from your Aunt?"

"No not yet but I should probably be heading back, I know they are suppose to be discharging her today."
Zaron sighed and said,

"I've really enjoyed spending time with you, hate you have to leave."

"I do too." I looked over at Zaron as he walked towards me and kissed me on the cheek.

"I've been running as you can see, I'm going to get cleaned up then I can take you back by the hospital."

"That's a good idea, you are all sweaty."

"Oh… I'm too sweaty for you." Zaron said laughingly as he hugged me from behind.

"Did you forget, I'm wearing your robe? You aren't making me sweaty you are really just funking your robe up." "Aww man," Zaron said and we both laughed as he ran upstairs.

November 15, 2015

Around 12pm the doctor cleared Aunt Macie to be discharged from the hospital.

"How are you feeling?" The doctor asked.

"I'm still very sore," Aunt Macie replied.

"Yes, you will be sore for a while, just continue taking your pain medication and take it easy for the next six weeks." The doctor explained. I grabbed our bags and headed to the car. I wasn't looking forward to the long drive home.

Chapter Twelve

June 17, 2014

As I stood in the living room I glanced around. Looking at family pictures, drawings from the kids, the furniture and all of our possessions. I glanced down at a nice fluffy white blanket, lying on the sofa, that we all used to snuggle under to watch a movie. I glanced at the board games that we played as a family. I walked into the kitchen, reminisced of making cookies with the kids. Cooking dinner for my family. Attempting to plan outings and dinner dates for my husband & I on many occasions and him not being available because of his so called church duties. The more and more I reminisced the worst and worst I felt. Boxes filled the rooms, Jasper had been gone for about three weeks, he moved in with his lover and was still preaching at the church. Loneliness is a bitch. I felt so betrayed, not only by him but by the church as well. All I constantly think about is how I have failed myself. "Why must I endure such pain?" I said as I walked through my house. I walked over to my storage rack, I still hadn't packed my records, I took out Albert King's I'll play the blues for you and placed it on the record player. As the music played I stood up and began dancing. I let the music take me away from this place. It soothed my soul and made love to my ears all while hugging my mind and kissing my lips. All the instruments impacted my being and medicated my body, especially my heart. I took a seat on the couch in the living room. Took a deep breath and looked up at the ceiling and just thought. I stayed in that position for about fifteen minutes until I heard a bird chirping on the windowsill. I glanced over. It was a blue jay. I watched it prance around and chirp until it flew away. "Its time for you to fly now Paris." I thought to myself. "Get your shit together and get the fuck out of here with your head held high." "Your kids love you, and you love yourself…. Right… Don't you Paris?" I shrugged my shoulders and stood up from the couch and walked over to the window. The clouds painted the skies in wisps of delight.

"There's got to be something better. I continued to packing. I heard a knock on the door.

"Who's there?"

"Its me, Angie. I have cake and champagne." I opened the door.

"What's the occasion?"

"We are celebrating your new start!" Angie said. I looked at her with tears in my eyes. "Really, Come in." Angie smiled and made her way to the kitchen.

"You haven't packed all of the silverware yet have you?"

"I think I still have a few pieces out on the counter. I'll grab a knife so we can cut the cake. Oh, and a couple of champagne flutes."

"So… Where are you moving?

"Well I have family in Greensboro, North Carolina. So, I'm moving back home so to speak."

"Back to our old stomping grounds." Angie said as she popped the champagne.

"Yeah I guess so. It's the most logical thing to do. The cost of living is much cheaper." I sliced the cake and had a taste.

"This cake is yummy! What is it?"

"It's white cake with strawberries and blueberries with a vanilla bean ganache icing. I knew you'd love it!"

"Yes, I like, I love."

"Paris you know this is just a small rough patch don't give up on love ok."

"I hear you." I said as I rolled my eyes.

"How is the job search going?"

"How are you and Jose?" I said.

"We're good. Things are progressing. We have been keeping in contact." Angie said as she smiled and blushed.

"Oh my! I see you are very sweet on him. I haven't seen you smile this much ever."

"Whatever Paris, stop trying to change the subject. Are you looking for another job?"

"Yes, I've found three good prospects. I've submitted my applications and now I'm just waiting to hear back from them."

"Look at you. Always in survival mode."

"Life has a way of making you survive."

"You should try law enforcement." Angie said as we looked at one another and laughed.

"I wouldn't last a day."

Angie and I finished our slices of cake and glasses of champagne. I turned on some Duke Ellington jazz music.

"I've been looking for a condos in Greensboro. I found a very nice one downtown. Its brand new and I think I'm going to buy it. Oh and its right above a spicy hot new restaurant. So if I don't feel like cooking the kids and I can just eat downstairs."

83

"Convenient." Said Angie.

"Yes, very convenient, I am all about convenience and easy stress free living."

"Have you talked with Jasper since he left?"

"No, I haven't heard from him since."

"So he gets caught sleeping with his guy friend and he doesn't try to get you back, apologize, or anything?"

"Nope."

"Ok I need another glass of champagne." Angie said. I laughed. It was good to finally be able to laugh at the situation rather than sulk and cry.

"Oh, gal we haven't played cards in a while. Can you still play?"

"Oh, you trying to play me. Now you know I still got it." I said as I grabbed the deck of cards I had thrown in a box.

"Lets play a game or two of Spades tonight."

"Bet."

Angie and I played a few games and drank all the champagne. As we finished up our last game I looked up at Angie and said,

"I'm really gonna miss ya girl."

"I'm going to miss you too."

Chapter Thirteen

June 18, 2014 10:00AM

"Good morning, & thank you for coming Paris, I know this must be hard for you considering your profession and education experience but I think this is going to help you," Dr. Monzingo said while making some notes in her tablet.

"Good morning, yes, I did find it quite difficult coming in but I know that I need to do this. This is just one of many steps I have to take in order to move forward in my life." I glanced around my psychiatrist office. It was very cozy and warm. She had this spectacular picture of the ocean horizon that was nicely grazed with floating clouds above the water. I looked deeply into the picture and kinda lost myself.

"Paris… Paris, are you ok? Do you need me to repeat the question?"

"Yes, I'm sorry I didn't hear you."

"How do you feel about yourself?" "Take as much time as you need too to answer the question, ok." She said while looking down at her notebook. Thinking about my life, my marriage, and the complete situation caused nothing but heartache and depression.

"I feel like giving up." I said as tears ran down my cheeks. "I don't know what I did to deserve this, this treatment." "I feel so stupid for believing someone when they told me they loved me." "I feel so stupid for trusting someone." "I feel that my marriage was a lie, it was for show, I was used as a cover up." "There have been times when I just sit at home in the dark and cry." "I can normally pull myself together for my children but they have seen me broken and at my worst." "I don't want to put them through this anymore." "I just want to stop crying, stop feeling."

"Paris, these are normal feelings for a person to have that has experienced such heartache as you have." Dr. Monzingo said as she handed me a few tissues. "This will eventually pass but want I want you to know is that you have to be strong to endure the pain." "Don't give up." "One day you will look back on this situation and pain will not be as intense as it is now." "Maybe one day the pain will go away maybe not." "Paris, I know you are a first lady in a very well known church." "How does that weigh in on the way you feel?" Dr. Monzingo asked. I could feel my eye begin to twitch. It would always twitch when I felt overwhelmed. My heart began to beat faster and I started to feel as if I couldn't breath.

"It weighs heavily on how I feel. I feel as if I have let so many people down that may look at our relationship and be inspired that they will one day find love and have a God fearing family." "I feel bad for wanting a divorce but I also feel that I cannot stay in a loveless, lifeless, abusive marriage." I wiped my eyes, which by now were red and covered with specks of tissue paper.

"I also feel embarrassed. My faith is completely gone." "I'm angry with God." "I feel that God has forsaken me." "I don't want to even hear anything about God or the church." "I can honestly say that this entire experience has made me hate church. I know not everyone is a bad person but I just don't want to go to a place where the members lie, backstab you, and are total hypocrites." "I tried to confide in one of his friends who is married to my friend and you know what he tried to do... He tried to get with me." "So unbelievable." "I must be the most naive person in the world." I cried as I shook my head.

"No you aren't naive, you are just learning how the world can be." "So Paris is this the main reason you wanted the divorce or were there other reasons?"

"No, there were other reasons, but I was determined to stick it out and make it work until the day I found out he was gay." "The first year of our marriage was ok, but it wasn't a normal newly wed year. We rarely had sex and when we did it really wasn't good. He never really said sweet things to me anymore; that totally stopped. I would cook but he wouldn't compliment my food. He wouldn't even have a conversation with me. He was always working for the church." "Church was first in his book." "It was so bad that he would just text me his schedule for the week." "Ha, I can remember receiving a text message for two weeks out that stated what he was doing for the church every day, no time set aside for family at all." "I couldn't even get a decent hug." "All I wanted was for him to love me and show me." "Oh, well, I guess I was asking for too much." I looked over at my Dr. and she was crying.

"Paris, I've tried to hold back my tears but I understand how you feel. It's ok to cry. Let it out."

"That's my problem, I can't stop."

"Have you had any thoughts of suicide?" Dr. Monzingo asked. I shook my head yes.

"I've had thoughts, when I got married I wanted it to be my only marriage."

"Its not your fault that he wasn't honest with you from the beginning." She exclaimed. I took a deep breath.

"Let me get you a glass of water, I'll be right back."

"Thank you." I looked in my purse, found small compact mirror, took a look at my face. My face was so puffy and swollen." I feel so weak, is what I thought to myself. I am an educated woman, why do I need to be here spilling my life to some stranger. She returned to the room with a tall glass of iced water.

"Thank you!" I gulped the water down.

"Feeling better?" Dr. Monzingo asked.

"Yes, thank you."

"I do have one more question I'd like to ask you and I want your complete honesty," she said as she sternly looked at me.

"Ok," I answered.

"What types of suicide thoughts have you had? Please know that this information is confidential. I just want to know if you have actually made plans, or if you are just saying that you want or wanted to end your life."

"I've actually thought of possible ways to end it." The doctor nodded her head up and down. Then said,

"I'd like to continue our sessions at least for the next six months. I'm going to prescribe you some medication to help with the crying spells and the depression." "This medication can be very addictive and is not meant for long-term use." "It will at least allow you to continue living, taking care of your kids, working successfully. One thing you don't want to do is lose absolutely everything you've worked for."

"Thanks so much. I actually feel a little better already." I grabbed my purse and began to stand up.

"Please stop by the front desk and schedule your next appointment about one month out with the receptionist." "I look forward to seeing you again, hopefully much happier."

I smiled and walked out of her office and down the hall to the receptionist. It felt good to let it all out.

Chapter Fourteen

December 2, 2015

Ring… Ring… I heard my phone ringing but couldn't remember where I placed it. I had just finished a very important detailed meeting at work that ran over. It was 5:40pm and I was supposed to meet Jasper at my place by 5:30pm so I could get Joii.

"Shit… I'm going to be late." I said to myself. Ring… Ring… My phone started ringing again. I shuffled around some papers on my desk and found it underneath.

"Hello" I answered.

"Hello, where are you at?" Shouted Jasper. I began to shake and tremble.

"Jasper I am running late, I apologize give me twenty minutes and I will be right there."

"No I'm leaving you will just have to pick her up next week."

"Jasper please I want to see my daughter."

"You better get here fast." Jasper disconnected the phone call. I could tell Jasper was on edge so I decided to swing by my mother's house and pick her up so I would have someone at home with me when I met him. We pulled up and I parked in one of my designated parking spaces. I rang Jasper. He answered, "Ok, I'm here, I will buzz you up." I said as my mother and I walked into my place. My mother took a seat. I placed my purse on the dining room table.

"Ma can you please get the door when he comes."

"No Paris, you can answer it, you guys are going to have to learn to work together."

"Ma, please get the door, Jasper is very angry with me still about the separation."

"No, I honestly don't want to deal with him myself. He is one disrespectful man." My mother said & I couldn't blame her for feeling that way. Jasper held something against women every since his mother passed away. He could never bond with my mother no matter how nice she was to him. Hell, he couldn't even bond with me. He got along much better with his male friends. Knock… knock… knock… I heard him at the door. I walked to the door and opened it.

"Mommy!" Joii yelled. Jasper handed her to me.

"Hi sweetheart. I've missed you so." I gave her a big hug and put her down so she could go see her grandma.

"She needs to use the bathroom Paris."

"Ok, I will ensure she goes to the bathroom."

"She needs to use it NOW!"

"Look Jasper you need to stop trying to be so controlling. We are no longer together. You chose who you wanted as a confident. Joii is with me now and I will make sure she uses the bathroom." I started to close the door, I looked down and saw that Jasper stuck his foot in.

"What is your problem? I tried to slam the door closed but Jasper began to push from the other side. He was much stronger than I was. "BAAMMMM" he kicked the door in and it flew off the hinge, then he stepped inside of my home. I glanced up and saw my mother run to one of the back rooms with Joii.

"Call the cops!" I screamed. I was stuck behind the door. Jasper grabbed the door and pulled it off of me. Placed his hands around my neck and jerked me from the floor.

"I cant... breathe" I mumbled. Jasper's face was intensified in anger and he looked as if he truly wanted me dead. "I... can't... breathe..." the words barely escaped my lips. Jasper finally let go after about 15 seconds. He backed away from me and looked at me as I gasped for air.

After I was able to catch my breath I yelled, "Gettt Outtt!" Jasper just stood there frozen. "Leave, just leave." I screamed. Jasper looked around at the devastation he caused, turned around and left. I ran to the bathroom. Too ashamed to have my mother and kids see me in such devastation. After all I was superwoman to my children. That very moment just brought all of the heartache back. Thinking back on when we first separated, sitting on the couch in the living room after I had pack up items, taken down pictures, seeing the rooms that were once filled with love and wonderful memories burned by lies and deception. Feeling empty and alone in a huge house that didn't feel like home. I sat on the couch and just… cried, couldn't stop the tears no matter how hard I tried to. My children watched me and knew that I was hurting but also knew that there wasn't anything they could do to help me. I can remember perfectly looking up at my son with tears streaming down my face and he looked directly in my eyes, placed his little hand on my shoulder and said, "Don't cry mom, I'm sorry." I didn't think I could have ever been hurt as much as I was during that time. I never thought I would be in such pain to need to be consoled by my child.

I sat in my bathroom on toilet with the water running to drown out my sobs and try to come back to reality. Trying to avoid insanity and live my life I picked myself up, walked back into the living room where the front door was knocked off the hinges and partly on the floor. I called to file a police report, not to get my ex locked up but so I had proof as to what did happen.

"Damn, its gonna cost me an arm and a leg to fix this door!" I yelled, mad at God… I thought to myself, "Why… Why do I have to go through this." I am one of the nicest, loving, giving, person one could know. This entire situation has me hating God, Christians, church, religion, everything for so many reasons.

Chapter Fifteen

December 31, 2015

I contemplated if I would celebrate New Years Eve. The holidays this year have been the loneliest and saddest that I've ever experienced in my life. I felt very confused considering that this year brought considerable pain and heartache. I decided to stay in and watch the ball drop in Times Square New York on TV with the kids.

"Mom when is the New Year coming in?" Asked Simone.

"Well, its about ten til eleven right now so it should be here within the next hour, do you think you will be able to stay up?"

Simone giggled, and said, "I think so." Then she took off down the hall.

"Simone, you can sit on the couch with me if you want to." I shouted.

"Alright, I'm coming, just gonna get my baby doll."
Simone made her way back in to the living room and took
a seat right beside me. After an hour had passed by I
looked over at Simone and she had fallen asleep. "Let me
put her in the bed" I said, as I stood up from my comfy
sofa and carried my daughter to bed. I noticed Sammie had
also fallen asleep playing his XBox. I shook my head that
little boy loves that Xbox.

"Guess I'll just bring the New Year in by myself." I
said as I walked back into the living room with about three
minutes to spare until the clock struck midnight. Then I
heard a knock on my door… "Who could this be," I
thought to myself as I walked to my door. I looked
through the peephole in my door; it was Zaron. I'd notice
those eyes from a mile away. He was smiling and holding a
vase filled with beautiful flowers.

"Oh my God, what is he doing here?" I whispered.
My hair was wrapped up. All I could think about is how
awful I looked. I had on some nicely fitted gray sweat
pants and a Pittsburg Steelers tee shirt. I opened the door.

"Hello."

"Hi Paris, I know you are surprised to see me. I don't
normally do the pop up thing but I just had to see you.
These are for you." He handed me the beautiful bouquet
of Lilies and Peonies.

"Come in." Zaron walked in. He looked so damn good. Smelled so damn good. I closed the door, placed the flowers on the table, when I turned around Zaron grabbed me around my waist, pulled me in towards him, looked me in my eyes and kissed me deeply. I had to pull away just to catch my breath. His lips passionately caressed mine, then I felt him slide his tongue into my mouth. My tongue intertwined with his. The chemistry and passion was definitely there. I could feel his lips move slowly from my mouth to my neck then up to my ear. He swiftly picked me up and headed down the hall. We made eye contact and I said,

"It's the last door on the right." Once inside he lied me down on the bed. As I gazed into his eyes he pulled my shirt up and over my head, then tugged my sweat pants down. I was already bra-less. Bending over he started pulling my lace panties down with his teeth; once he got them past my hips he used his hands to slowly take them off.

"You are beautiful. I want you to be mine." He said as he kissed my forehead, then my nose, then my lips, making his way to my neck I felt his hand rubbing my clit. I let out a pleasurable moan. His sexy lips found my plump round breast, where he spent some time sucking my nipples until I couldn't take it any longer,

"Oh God," I wailed. Zaron looked up then slowly made his way down to my toned abs kissing and licking the indentions of my sides then teased me with his tongue until he found my clit. Opening his mouth he devoured my pussy. Licking my clit and inside my vagina until I reached indescribable ecstasy. I tried to close my legs,

"Un uh, give me this pussy" I began to relax, grabbed his head and pulled him deeper into me. Breathing harder and harder I murmured,

"Oh, Zaron… I'm about… to…" "Ahhhhh, ahhhh, Zay, that feels so good." I released and Zarons's mouth was covered in my juices, he stood up leaned in and gave me a kiss.

"That's my pussy!"

"Yes baby, its yours." I said, as his lips covered mine, we continued insatiable kisses; with my heart pounding I pushed him away. I sat up slowly and unbuttoned his shirt, pulled his tie to loosen it up a little and slid his shirt off of his body.

"Give me some of that booty." Zaron said as he flipped me over onto my stomach. He devoured my groceries.

"Damn baby… I can't keep any groceries in this house." I said. Zaron had been back there for a while & I couldn't deny that it felt sooooo good! After he finished he turned me back over. He stood there looking at me like a lion looks at his prey right before he pounces on it, grabbing it and never letting go, devouring it until he is full. He slowly came out of the trance I had him in and tugged his pants and boxers down then kicked them away. Climbing on top of me we kissed passionately, I could feel his soul connect with mine. Wrapping his arms around me he squeezed me, holding me tight and looking deeply into my eyes as he entered my wet place. He moaned with satisfaction.

"Shit! Oh God," I moaned. He stroked me slowly, over and over and over again. Allowing my pussy to relax in total satisfaction. The way he caressed my wet place brought out some many emotions for him and I. I continued to feel him grow inside of me, filling me completely, his long dick & long strokes massaging my G-spot; I began to shake and drip with wetness. I could no longer control myself, he could no longer hold back, we both climaxed together, as my pussy gripped his pulsating dick he filled me.

"Aaaahhhhhh, ahhhhh, babe." Zaron let out deep moans, wrapped me up in his arms and hugged me tight. "Happy New Year." Zaron said. A few minutes later we fell fast asleep.

Chapter Sixteen

Friend Love

I want you, & I know you want me, my friend

Unexplainable

My friend

The feelings that I have inside

Of my mind

For you

My friend, my friend

But you're just a friend

The chemistry

Between you and me

It's like lightening

Jagged yet so defined

You jolt me with a spark inside

Quivering feels so damn divine

Hold me, Rock me, Fuck me, Choke me

Hold me, Rock me, Fuck me, Love me

Love me, Love me, Love me, Love me… Kiss me…

Friend

Just to feel you run your fingers down my spine

Just to feel your fingers going inside

Just to feel your lips caressing mine

My friend… My friend

Just to feel you run your fingers down my spine

Just to feel you going inside

Just to feel your lips caressing mine

My Friend… Friend

And when I feel

You between my thighs

I am lost

In The depth of the sea in your eyes

So deep, calming

Soothing, dreamy, loving, dirty, freaky, sexy

Hold me, Rock me, Fuck me Choke me

Hold me, Rock me Fuck me Love me

Love me, Love me, Love me, Love me… Kiss me…

Friend…

Chapter Seventeen

March 12, 2016

I found a street parking space near the Dame's Chicken & Waffles off of Martin Luther King Drive in downtown Greensboro. It was around 10:30am and the rain was pouring down. Bradd had invited me to breakfast. It had been a while since I seen him considering his lack of interest in the relationship. I was dressed in a pencil red skirt and a ruffle white blouse. I put on my Jessica Simpson black pumps with a silver watch and earrings to accent the outfit. I reached in my mini Coach purse and pulled out my favorite perfume, You & I by One Direction, sprayed a couple pumps on my neck and wrist. I threw on my black posh shades, stepped out of my BMW and began walking to the entrance of the restaurant. A large muscular man, with curly black hair, greeted me.

"Good morning Ma'am" he said, as he looked me up and down. I just stood there waiting for him to finish making whatever observation he was making.

"I'm actually meeting someone and I see he is sitting right over there." I took my shades off and slightly pointed at Bradd.

"Right this way." The host said as he seated me at the table with Bradd.

"Good Morning Mrs. James."

"Bradd"

"How was the drive over here."

"Well you know I live like five minutes away. It wasn't bad at all."

"How have you been?"

"I've been doing good actually."

"Hey I'm sorry about getting missing. Dating a woman with kids is new for me."

"Its cool."

"Ready to order."

"Ummm… Sure, I know exactly what I want" I said as Bradd motioned for the waitress to come to our table. We ordered and had a very lengthy discussion.

"Mrs. James, I get the feeling that you aren't exactly ready for what I am ready for."

"And what exactly is that Bradd?"

"The getting to know a guy process."

"Bradd I think we both have different definitions of the "Getting to know a guy process." Your definition of it is having sex without the intention of a relationship for possibly years without a commitment. No true or real communication and no emotional connection. Women are emotional beings. I need to have that emotional connection with you." "My definition of the getting to know a guy process is just that. Getting to know him. Seeing where he is mentally and what stage he is at in his life, which would of course, determine if he wants a relationship. My observation of you is just that. You only want a hang out boo. Unfortunately that's not me especially if you only want casual sex and conversation"

"If that's how you feel Mrs. James."

"Its how I feel Bradd."

"Are you talking to someone else?"

"I've recently found someone."

The waitress bought our food and we ate and shared a few laughs. I looked closer into Bradd's eyes and I saw a new pain.

"My uncle passed away a few weeks ago."

"I'm so sorry to hear that Bradd." I grabbed his hand.

"I wish you would have told me sooner, I really wish I could have been there for you."

"I know I've got to work on my communication Paris. Kids also make me nervous."

"I kinda figured they did since you never wanted to include them. It's cool. No worries."
I looked up at Bradd and smiled. He smiled back then said,

"I'm still hungry, think I need to order another dish."
We both laughed. Bradd loved to eat.

"That was delicious."

"Yes it was. What do you have planned for the day Mrs. James?"

"Taking the kids to the movies then later I'm attending a poetry event."

"That sounds interesting. I hope you enjoy your day. "I'll walk you to your car."
Bradd walked me to my car and kissed me on my forehead. It was still raining as I sat in my car and thought about the conversation we had just had. After a few minutes I received a text message from Bradd. It read,

Thanks for meeting me today. I miss you already. Most guys don't realize what they have until its gone.

 I placed my phone back in my purse and drove off. I thought to myself, sometimes things work out and sometimes they don't but its ok. It's life.

My 1000 Piece Puzzle

Differences within each individual

Make them who they are

Size, shape, age, race

Culture, origin and sex

It takes time to put all of these pieces together

In ones particular order,

Do I hate myself, no, I love myself, but do I really know

myself?

No one person can put

The pieces of their puzzle together alone

Your puzzle is an effect of

Each person that has pierced your life

Anger, love, laughter, fear

Your life is precious

Treat it as such

Saving yourself heartache

Not shielding yourself so

That you miss out

Find your puzzle and complete it

Chapter Eighteen

February 14, 2016 Valentines Day

My body was wrapped in a plush white towel, I had just stepped out of the bathtub and water droplets were still on my brown skin. I walked over to the living room I gazed out of my floor to ceiling windows. Downtown Greensboro was full and vibrant. Couples lined the streets to celebrate Valentines Day. It was a dark night and the sky was full of stars.

"Oooo" I said as I looked up into the sky.

"A shooting star!" I'd never seen one of those before, I had only read about them or saw them on TV. Just the sight of it felt exhilarating. I glanced at the clock, it was 6pm and I needed to get ready for my date with Zaron. I had pondered a few different outfits to wear. One of them was deep purple with a low front that plunged down to show a lot of cleavage. The next one was a deep dark red semi sparkling fitted dress that was backless, The last outfit that I had also liked was a white chiffon top with white wide legged dress pants that flowed in chiffon to match. I went to the salon earlier in the day and had my stylist to spiral curl my hair. After glamorizing my makeup I turned on my speakers and played my favorite love playlist, which consisted of Musiq Soulchild, Ne-yo, Raheem Devaughn & D'Angelo. They all create music with a meaning. To me there is nothing better than a song that has the ability to touch your soul and feel it emotionally because you relate to it on such a high level.

As I put on my outfit I heard my doorbell ring. I answered the door. There stood Zaron in a black tuxedo with a red tie and a red handkerchief.

"For you pretty face. Happy Valentine's Day" He pulled a dozen red roses from behind him. My face lit up.

"Thank you, they are gorgeous! Happy Valentines Day to you as well." I smelled my roses and smiled. I placed them on the island in the kitchen. Zaron took my hand in his and we headed out the door and to the elevator.

"Where are we going?" I asked.

"Follow me sweetie." He replied. We walked downtown for a couple of blocks then crossed the street at East February 1 Place.

"Churchill's on Elm.'

"Yes, have you ever been here before?"

"No, never been here."

"Good!"

"Is that good? I stay downtown and rarely have time to get out and experience life."

"It just gives me the chance to take you out more." He chuckled and I laughed. They had special guests performing for the evening. We were sat at a small table for two in the middle of the restaurant. We ordered a bottle of Rose and an appetizer of broiled oysters and spinach dip. There was an acquired aroma of cigars and beer in the air, which smelled lovely. The place was filling up. I'm sure since it was Valentines Day they were booked with reservations. The owner came out and took the stage.

"Good evening everyone. We have a very special guest in the building tonight to help you share in celebrating this very special Valentine's Day. Everyone please welcome K-Ci & JoJo!" The host said as they took the stage. I turned and looked at Zaron.

"This is amazing."

"Anything for you." Zaron shared as he kissed my cheek. We sat and listened to an abundance of classic songs, danced, shared in our food and drinks. Zaron placed his hand on mine at the table. I looked up after placing an oyster in my mouth.

"Lets make this official." Zaron said. "I know we have been dating but we haven't officially said or told anyone else that we are in a relationship." "I'm ready for that, are you?"

"I'm ready." After gazing into each other's eyes we locked lips and shared a very deep passionate kiss that lasted what seemed to be a forever.

"I love you."

The show ended around eleven that night. We walked back to my condo. We could barely keep our hands to ourselves. Once inside I dimmed the foyer lights.

"Wait here, I'm going to change." I walked into my kitchen and found a lighter. I lit a few candles then went into my room to change. I had gone lingerie shopping earlier in the day and found a pink colored Chantilly lace plunge teddy. After putting it on I looked at myself in the mirror.

I slowly walked down the hall back into the living room. I heard some nice jazz playing. "Zaron must have found us something to listen to..." I thought to myself. When I entered Zaron's eyes widened.

"You took care of me earlier tonight, now I'm going to take care of you." I said as I slowly walked to my man.

"Lets take this off." I said as I aggressively loosened his tie and unbuttoned his shirt. Pulled his shirt off then got down on my knees and proceeded to un-do his belt and unbutton his dress pants. I slid them down his thighs.

"Have a seat" I said softly. Zaron took a seat down on the couch. I leaned in and gently kissed my man, absorbing all of him. I took a seat upon him and felt his manhood, which was extremely hard. I rubbed my pelvic area back and forth while teasing his ear. I know he could feel that I was wet. He had such an affect on me. I ran my tongue up and then down his earlobe. I applied soft tender kisses to his neck. Gave his nipples a little attention too then got down on my knees, looked him directly in the eyes and began sucking his dick. He had a long thick hard light brown dick and I savored every inch. I locked my plump juicy lips around his magic wand and sucked with every motion. I licked up all premature juices and continued to suck away. Before he could reach a magical climax I moved down towards his balls and licked and sucked them, giving them as much attention as needed. He tasted amazing. While making eye contact I placed his huge cock back into my mouth and began sucking again. Giving him total control he placed his hands on my head and pushed down so hard and fast I could feel him go past the back of my throat. Without gaging I continued to give him total control.

"I'm… about… to cum" He said as he gasps for air and let out a loud wail. I swallowed him aggressively ensuring to not let any of him go to waste. Zaron took me in his arms and kissed me passionately. Picked me up sat me on the kitchen island and entered me slowly. My vagina was tight and I felt him penetrate every inch of me. I tried to back away but his arms had me locked in. I let out a deep low moan of pain and satisfaction. His dick was a missing piece to my puzzle, and it fit perfectly. He moved back and forth, up and down slowly for a long time. We gazed into each other's eyes. While sharing loving kisses the motion of his dick caused me to reach the highest climax. I couldn't hold back my release any longer. I felt him throb inside of me, releasing all of his love. I began to squirt all over him. He took pleasure in making me loose all control and tremble uncontrollably. My body went limp. Zaron carried me to the bedroom and we both fell asleep cuddled in one another's arms.

Chapter Nineteen

September 17,2016

"You ready bae?" Zaron shouted.

"Yeah, I'm ready... I'm comin." I yelled from the bathroom. I had surprised Zaron with tickets to the Virginia Tech football game. They were playing my team the Duke Blue Devils at the Lane Stadium in Blacksburg Virginia today. Zaron was and has always been crazy about the Hokies. We were headed up with my good friends Meagan & her boyfriend Jason. They both were of Caucasian decent. Meagan was very slender with blonde hair and pretty blue eyes. Jason was tall and slim with dirty blond hair, grey eyes and a rugged beard. They had been in a relationship for about 7 years. Meagan had discussed with me how she was ready for marriage and kids but Jason wasn't.

"Bae… your phone is ringing, again. It's Meagan. Want me to answer it?"

"Yes."

I heard Zaron as he answered my phone. I hurriedly finished applying my mascara, tugged my Nike Air Max's on and scurried into the kitchen.

"Dimples, they are outside waiting on us to head down."

"Ok, I'm ready let me just grab the bag of snacks I made us. Will you grab the beer and the cooler? I said. Dimples' was a nickname that Zaron started calling me because he said my face was so pretty but my dimples were absolutely gorgeous. We headed downstairs and met up with our friends.

"Alright, who is driving first?" Jason said.

"Jason… Really… We all know that more than likely you and Zaron will be totally wasted when the game is over. How about you guys drive up and we will drive back?" I suggested.

"That works for me!" Zaron said as he looked over at Jason and shrugged his shoulders.

"Sure." Jason said as he pulled out a cigarette. "The tank is full so we shouldn't have to fill up again until the game is over."

The terrain going up to Blacksburg Virginia was gorgeous. We decided to take the back roads instead of the interstate. The land was filled with hills, cliffs, and green pastures. We passed by a small little country store and picked up a few things. About 45 minutes after we left the store Jason said,

"I'm going to swing by my parents house really quickly so we can pick up our tickets. We are about 10 minutes from their house and they stay about 30 minutes away from the stadium."

"Good cause I've got to use the potty." I said.

"I do too!" said Meagan.

After a long ride we finally made it to Blacksburg Virginia. Found a parking space off of Harrell Street and made our way down towards the stadium. On our way there we passed by a white frat house packed with students; which appeared to be swaying it was so full and they were so hype. We had already been drinking the entire way up so we weren't quite sure if it was them or us swaying. When we arrived we were completely lit and ready for the game. Zaron took my hand in his as we walked through the crowd. It was a bright hot sunny day. There was a slight breeze in the air causing the leaves to flow on their branches. I had on a burnt orange halter top and some dark blue shorts, Zaron had actually taken of his white tee and only had on his blue shorts. We were already sweating from the extreme heat but luckily we had a cooler full of sports drinks, water and beer. Zaron leaned in and kissed me on the cheek. That's just was one example of why I loved this man, even though I had never actually told him. He was extremely affectionate, trust worthy, honest and showed sincere concern about my wellbeing. These were all traits that I needed in a partner. I am not one to take the "love" word lightly. After my ex-husband, I never felt that I would be able to show love to anyone again. I know I'll tell him when the time is right.

We finally made it to the stadium and took our seats. The sun was beaming down on us. The band lined the field and everyone was standing up in the stands shouting, "Hokies, Hokies, Hokies." The band played and the football team stormed the field. The crowd went bananas & so did we! We had already had a few beers and were ready to see which team would win.

The game had been going for a little over three hours. The score was 37-43 with Virginia leading. Snyder from Duke caught the football for a touch down causing the game to go into overtime.

"Ok, Jason, Virginia has got to pull this off." Said Zaron.

"Oh we are going to win this, we've got to!" exclaimed Jason.

"Sounds to me like you guys are getting nervous. I think Duke will win this, I mean Snyder has been giving it his all during this game." I said.

"We will see," said Zaron.
It was overtime and Duke had the ball. All they need is a touch down and a two-point conversion to win the game. Sirk landed the two-point conversion and it was all over.

"Yay!" Meagan and I screamed! We were elated that our team had won. As Zaron and Jason picked their faces up from the ground we packed up our stuff and headed out. It was dark and we were hungry.

"Aye what's a good place to eat at up here?" said Zaron.

"There is this steakhouse not too far from here, we can stop there and eat then head to the hotel." said Jason. We had booked a hotel about an hour away so when we left in the morning it wouldn't take us that long to get back home.

"Who's driving…?" We all looked at each other in silence, "Ok I'll drive." Meagan said as we walked back to the car.

We arrived at Texas Roadhouse and was seated near the bar area. A waiter came us to our table and asked what we would like to drink.

"I'll have a pitcher of Miller Lite." And a couple shots of Jack Daniels Tequila for all of us" said Zaron.

"That works for me" said Jason. Meagan and I nodded in agreement. The waiter wrote down our orders and went to the bar.

"Ok, so have you all given any thought to this presidential election? I mean we are all close friends and we shouldn't feel uncomfortable discussing this. I honestly do not know who I'm going to vote for." I murmured.

"I think this is going to be one of the closest and most confusing elections in history. I mean we all want change but at what cost?" Meagan added.

"I'm a Trump supporter myself, said Jason. I want change; I'm tired of the same ole stuff going on. He would be like a breath of fresh air you know."

"Maybe." I said.
The waiter arrived with our drinks and we placed our food orders.

"Paris you are up next to drive, don't forget we still need to stop and get gas." Jason said.
I looked around and saw that the restaurant was packed. More and more people were coming in from the game I

119

suppose. The kitchen was really moving and we were able to get our food in no time. We had a very pleasant time, good food and good laughs. We headed out to the car so we could get to the hotel and get some sleep. We all were very tired. I hopped in the drivers seat backed out of the parking space. We embarked through some of the back roads that were very winding with extreme drop off cliffs. We were driving for about thirty minutes when the gas light came on.

"Uh... guys the gas light is on and I haven't seen a gas station in miles."

"Oh shit! I don't want to get stuck up here on this mountain in the dark & I'm drunk." Said Jason.

"Just drive baby until we come up on one, ok." Zaron said. I nodded yes and continued to drive. It was extremely dark outside and the moon was full. I turned on the radio and Keys to the Streets was on by YFN Lucci. I began dancing and took my eyes off the road for a split second. When I looked back up I saw something tall black and furry run across the road and slammed on the breaks and turned the car off.

"What the fuck is going on?" said Jason as he and Meagan looked at me and around the inside of the car. He grabbed the left side of his neck. His head slammed into the back of my seat when I slammed on the breaks.

"Paris, what's going on babe?"

"I think I just saw Big Foot."

"What? You just saw Big Foot." Said Jason. "Are you that drunk?" "Let me drive."

"I'm serious! I saw Big Foot." Zaron and Jason looked at me with a raised eyebrow puzzled look.

"I saw it too!" Meagan whispered. We all turned and looked at her.

"You did!" I said. "I know what I saw."

"Um, you guys don't look to your left because it's right outside your door Jason." Everyone slowly looked to their left.

"Ahhhhhhhhhhhhh." Every one screamed to the top of their lungs.

"Paris, crank up the car and lets get the fuck out of here." Jason exclaimed.
I tried turning the starter but the car wouldn't crank up.

"Keep trying." Zaron said
Big Foot had opened Jason's door. Jason pulled it back closed and yelled,

"Lock the doors, it's trying to get into the car." I locked the car doors and tried to crank the car up again. No luck.

"Give it some fucking gas!" yelled Jason who was pouring sweat by now. I tried again and the car finally crank up. I slammed my foot on the pedal and we flew down the hilly mountain. We continued driving for about 20 minutes when the car started to creep. The gas was almost gone.

"I think we are riding on fumes." I said

"No… We've got to make it to a gas station. Where are all the fucking gas stations?" Said Jason. We continued riding for about a minute when we rolled up on a closed gas station. The lights were out but I turned in anyway hoping that we could still use it. The car rolled in slow and then cut off right as I pulled beside a gas stall. We all jumped out the car. Zaron pulled a credit card out of his wallet. Then we all stared at one another hoping that it would take the card despite the store being closed. Zaron inserted his card and the machine lit up and accepted the payment.

"Thank you God! Said Jason. I hugged Meagan and we let out a big sigh of relief. Zaron filled the tank.

"What a night…" I said as I pulled off to head to the hotel.

Chapter Twenty

June 20, 2016

"All Rise, the Honorable Judge Inman Presided." The bailiff stated. Everyone in the courtroom stood up and in walked the Judge, whom was a tall Caucasian male, with grey hair. The judge took his seat. "You may be seated." The bailiff said.

"Today's divorce proceedings we have the case of James, vs. James." The judge said, then looked at my attorney.

"Are both parties present?"

"Yes both my attorney and Jasper's attorney stated."

"I have read over the case and it appears that the plaintiff Paris is requesting a divorce due to emotional alienation and infidelity and is also requesting spousal support, however the defendant Jasper denies the allegations but is not contesting the divorce just spousal support. You both have also been separated for at least a year. Is this correct?" The judge looked at Jasper's attorney.

"Yes this is correct," stated Jaspers attorney.

"Ok, why does the defendant want a divorce?"

"My client states that they have grown apart and he no longer wishes to be in the marriage," stated Jaspers attorney.

"And what exactly has caused them to grow apart?"

"My client is trying to find himself and his self identity. He realizes that he cannot be what the plaintiff needs and wishes to be divorced."

"Now you Mrs. James state that the defendant emotional alienated you and you also had to endure infidelity in the marriage. Is that correct?"

"Yes your honor. My client was emotionally alienated during the marriage and walked in on the defendant and his male friend sleeping together."

"Do you have proof?"

"Yes we have proof, we have text messages which confirm the defendant is gay and confirms the emotional alienation, but no direct proof of infidelity."

"Will you pass that up to me please." The judge stated. My attorney gathered the documents for the bailiff to hand to the judge. The judge looked over the documents for a while then asked.

"Are there any custody issues?"

"No," My attorney answered. "Both my client and the defendant have one child together and have agreed on joint custody."
The judge nodded his head.

"I'm going to grant the divorce and award spousal support in the amount of $1200 per month that will continue for a year. It is so ordered. Good luck to the both of you." The judge slammed his gavel down and the divorce was finalized. I took a deep breath and turned to my attorney who was very happy with the decision granted.

"You have a new start Paris." My attorney stated. "Good luck."

"Thank you" I said as I turned and walked out of the courtroom.

Chapter Twenty One

Options

Questions asked result in answers given

Decisions pondered result in options taken

Choices made define your future endeavors

Open minds create clarity within

Constant judgment of one's choices, can create insanity

Which is not an option available in your future

Winning should be the most logical option

Failure somehow sneaks it's way in if you let it

Procrastination creates havoc of devastation

Knowing in the end all that matters is you

Self made man, Aware of his options

Weighing his choices logically

Making decisions of clarity knowing

Winning is the only option in the end

Chapter Twenty Two

July 14, 2017

    Our plane landed at 4:10pm Friday evening. We finally arrived in New Orleans Louisiana. The weather was beautiful. It was a nice sunny day, about eighty degrees outside and there was a light breeze in the air. The tall palm trees swayed in the breeze. Zaron and I decided to plan a vacation with my best friend Angie and her boyfriend Jose. Since Angie still lived in Washington and Jose in the Outer Banks their flights were slightly longer than ours. Angie & Jose had really formed a long-lasting relationship from the time we vacationed in the Outer Banks a few years ago. Once outside of the airport we motioned for a taxi to take us to our hotel. We booked a week stay at Hotel Maison De Ville.

The taxi pulled in front of the hotel. The historic district of New Orleans had so much character. I loved the bold powerful colors of the mansions that lined the streets.

"It feels good to be back on the ground, that was a long flight." Said Angie as she turned around to allow Jose to rub her shoulders.

"Yes it was. I can't wait to experience this vacation with you," said Jose.

"These two little love birds," I said.

"Come on now Paris, you know you and I are the exact same. I can remember telling Paris how I didn't like public affection and I couldn't stand to see it but now I can't keep my hands off of her in public," said Zaron as I kissed him passionately and said,

"I think I found my soul mate.

"Damn gal can we at least get in the hotel. Y'all talking about Jose and I. I'd love to be a fly on the wall in your bedroom." Angie said as we all laughed. I turned to walk towards the hotel. I grabbed my purse and said, "First stop this evening, coffee and beignets, and all the cocktails I can consume. Oh and I can't wait for the festival tomorrow."

"I'm very excited about it too! Its all I've been thinking about for the past few weeks." Angie said.

"We will handle the check in and get the bags. Why don't you and Angie go have a seat in the lobby." Zaron said.

"Ok baby." I whispered as Angie and I walked in to the lobby area of the hotel. The hotel was very exquisite and unique. Located in the French Quarter of New Orleans it showcased its architecture throughout the entire hotel. We found a nice sofa in one of the main rooms and took a seat.

"How has life been in DC?"

"Life has been great. I've been promoted and have been able to solve many cases that were once cold." Angie said, as a cute little cat came and sat right beside us.

"That's awesome Angie! I'm so proud of you."

"Thank you Paris. I've missed having my best friend around."

"I've missed you too."

"The festival is tomorrow, what do you want to do this evening?"

"Beignets and coffee, Lets go get some after we settle in, around 8pm."

"That sounds good, I will check with Jose to see if he is up for it after the flight or if the men wanna just hang tonight then we can go together."

"Ok well I'll let you know what Zaron wants to do."

We saw the guys heading our way.

"Alright we are all set. We are in the Premium rooms right beside each other and we are sharing a balcony." Zaron said and he carried our luggage.

"This is going to be so much fun." I smiled and gazed at everyone. "We will get up with you all after we've settled in for a while."

"Ok" Angie and Jose said as they went to their room.

We opened our room door and were amazed at the history and architecture of the place. There was a beautiful chandelier that lit the room. It hang over a rose petal covered king sized bed. There was also a chilled bottle of champagne awaiting us. Zaron threw the bags down and hurriedly opened the bottle.

"Come here Paris." Zaron said as he poured the champagne into two glasses. "I want to make a toast to us. We both have been through a lot in the past and I want to make this toast to new beginnings and new life for the both of us." We both raised our glasses and drank the lovely champagne. With the bed being covered in roses Zaron took me in his arms and lay me down on the bed. He slowly undressed me taking off one piece of clothing at a time. It seemed like an eternity before I was completely naked. Zaron turned me around and pinned me down with my hands above my head, my face pressed into the pillows, back arched and booty in the air he entered me slowly.

"Ummmmmmm. Damn baby you make me feel so good."

"I love you dimples."

"I love you too."

My juices ran all over him, as he stroked me lovingly. Within minutes I felt him release.

"Ooooooo baby…" Zaron said as we both collapsed and fell fast asleep.

It was around 8:30pm when I heard a knock on the door. I grabbed the sheet from the bed and wrapped it around me. Zaron was still sleeping.

"Who is it?"

"Its me gal open this door."

"Um… I can't right now."

"What are y'all in there doing."

"Nothing now." I said laughingly

"Did you forget about beignets?"

"Oh I kinda did."

"Well Jose wants us all to go get some dinner. How does that sound."

"Ok that's cool. We will be down in the lobby in thirty."

"Ok." Angie said as she walked back to her room. I turned to walk towards the bed. I looked at Zaron and leaned down to give him a kiss on the cheek. "I'm about to get in the shower babe." Zaron looked up and said,

"I'm coming too."

"Naughty, naughty." I ran into the bathroom and bent over to turn on the shower. Zaron was directly behind me and I could feel his erection.

"Really babe. We just finished."

"I know but I want more." Zaron said as he turned me around towards him and kissed me. Kissing me up and down my neck, making his way to my breast and sucking my nipples until they became rock hard. I could feel the water run down my back. Zaron picked me up and entered me. I could feel him grown inside me. He held me and pounded me, just as the water pounded my back, I was stimulated all over.

"I'm addicted."

We all had our fill of fresh seafood. We were stuffed. After dinner we arrived back to the hotel, Zaron and Jose had picked up a pack of beers from the store and had headed up to the room balcony. Angie there is something that I need to talk to you about." I said as Angie made eye contact with me.

"What's going on? Are things ok with you and Zaron?"

"Yes Zaron and I are doing fine." I took a deep breath. "Angie it's something else. I think I may be pregnant."

"And that's a problem. I'm happy for you Paris."

"Thank you. It's just that Zaron and I have talked about how we both don't want any more children. Zaron especially."

"Well were you on any birth control."

"Yes, I was taking the birth control regularly and on time. I don't know what happened."

"Have you told him?"

"No, I don't want anymore and I know for a fact that he doesn't want any. I don't know what I'm going to do."

"How far along could you be?"

"I honestly don't know. My cycle isn't regular. I could be two months along…"

"Well you first need to take a pregnancy test. You said your cycles aren't regular. That is the only way to be sure. We can go out to the store and get a test tomorrow. I'm here for you Paris."

"Thank you"

The next day we attended the festival and we had a blast! We saw a variety of artists perform and had the time of our lives. Once the festival ended we headed back to the hotel by taxi. We were a couple of minutes from our hotel when Angie yelled.

"We will get out here."

"We will?" I said

"Yes remember you needed to stop by the store?"

"Oh. That's right. We will all get out here and walk back to the hotel." I said.

"What do you need from the store Paris?" Zaron asked.

"Oh just a few things, snacks and such." I said as Angie glared at me with a very puzzled look. The taxi driver let us out on Bourbon St. I found a small little store and ran in as Angie talked to Zaron and Jose.

"Get some chips babe." Zaron yelled as I walked into the store. I nodded my head.

"Ok, chips and a test." I said to myself. I was in the store no longer than about three minutes. I grabbed a big bag of barbeque chips and a pregnancy test.

"Oh that didn't take long at all. What did you get baby?" Zaron said as he grabbed the bag. "Just chips, I thought you wanted a few snacks?" I had stuffed the pregnancy test in my purse.

"Oh. I just wanted chips too." We all headed back to the hotel.

"We've got a surprise for you girls on the balcony, can you head on up and we will meet you out there?"

"Sure" I said, Angie and I went outside to the balcony and were surprised at the way it was decorated. It was lit up and covered in rose petals. There were four chairs and a couple of candles on the table that were lit. A nice bottle of champagne was on ice. We both took a seat. Jose came in and took a seat by Angie. Then in walked Zaron. Carrying a dozen of roses.

"These are for you sweet cheeks." I gasped at the beauty of the flowers. Paris we've known each other for years. In the more recent years I have grown to love you dearly. You complete me, you are the last piece to my puzzle." Zaron bent down on one knee and pulled out a small red box, he opened the box.

"Paris will you marry me sweetie?" Zaron said. I was in complete shock. I finally answered,

"Yes, yes I will marry you." Teary eyed I stood up and kissed my man. He took the ring out and placed it on my finger. "I can't wait to spend the rest of our lives together." Zaron said. The ring was a perfect fit.

We celebrated for most of the night. We danced and laughed and shared stories with our friends until about 3am in the morning. We both were very tired. Zaron had finally laid down to get some sleep after hours of making love. I decided that it was time to take the pregnancy test. I took the test in the bathroom, peed on it and waited. "Why am I so nervous?" I said to myself. I knew that Zaron didn't want to have any kids. He was ok with the three I had but didn't want any of his own. I sat on the toilet thinking of my past both the good and the bad. I stood up and picked up the test.

"Oh dear." It showed two pink lines.